SAVING

JIMMY

Other books by Linda Williams Jackson

THE LUCKY ONES (Candlewick)

MIDNIGHT WITHOUT A MOON (Clarion)

A SKY FULL OF STARS (Clarion)

SAVING

JIMMY

a work of fiction by award-winning author
Linda Williams Jackson

for

Jeff,

Olivia, Chloe, and Benjamin

always

CONTENTS

What's In a Name?

*"What's in a name? That which we call a rose by
any other name would smell as sweet."*
~ Romeo and Juliet

My name is Jimmy. I'm named after my daddy,
Jimmy Lee Johnson Jr.

My great-aunt Millie thinks it's a foolish name
for a girl. She says when a gum-smacking nurse laid
me on Mama's chest and asked, "So, sweetie, whatcha
gonna call her?" Mama smiled and answered, "Jimmy.
Just like her daddy."

Aunt Millie frowned and said, "Don't be a fool,
Darlynn. You can't have that gal going through life
with a boy's name."

But Mama just stared at her like she'd
swallowed a pickle and turned green.

"Why can't you call her Jenny?" Aunt Millie then asked. "Now that's a pretty name for a girl."

"Her name is Jimmy," Mama said, smiling proudly at the nurse.

The nurse winked at Mama and said, "What's in a name, right?"

But Aunt Millie glared at the nurse. "She could at least give that child a decent name. If nothing else."

"She's mine, and I'll call her what I want," Mama said. "Her name is Jimmy Lee Johnson."

Aunt Millie says the nurse looked at Mama real funny, then cleared her throat and said, "You can't name her that, sweetie." She looked toward the door real quick, then shook her head and said, "You can't name her Johnson."

So Mama named me Jimmy Lee Easton instead, giving me my daddy's first and middle name, and her last name. Aunt Millie was so mad that she stormed out of that hospital room and didn't say two words to Mama again until I was almost six months old.

That was twelve years ago. And Aunt Millie still barely has two words to say to Mama on any given day. Unless it's about God and Heaven. Or the devil and hell. Or who's going where. And how fast.

Of course, she says Mama's going straight to the hot place on account of her "riotous living." And since I'm twelve already ("The age of accountability," she says.), then I'd better hurry up and get it right with Jesus myself before it's everlastingly and eternally too late. Otherwise, I will end up there too.

But I don't have time to worry about Aunt Millie and her holy talk today. I've got more important things to think about, like getting glamorous for this field trip. Even if it means choking half to death on Pine-Sol, thanks to our custodian, Ms. Wicker. She won Custodian of the Year this week, so yesterday she outdid herself. The pine scent is so thick in this restroom this morning that you could cut it with a knife.

But I fight the stench and lean toward the squeaky-clean mirror anyway. I squint with one eye as I stroke Purple Passion over the other, carefully making a thin line across just like Danielle taught me. After both eyelids are satisfyingly purple, I curl my lashes with Thick Lush Mascara.

My best friend Danielle, the Queen of Makeup, smiles her approval.

Then comes the lip gloss.

Before I can get it on my lips good, Danielle frowns and yanks it from my hand, smearing it halfway across my face.

"Where were you when God was giving out lips?" she asks. She takes a tissue from her purse and starts scrubbing my lips like I just kissed a frog. "You got lip gloss everywhere, girl. I swear you got the weirdest shaped lips I ever saw."

I mumble through the tissue, "I don't get to practice all the time like you do."

I catch a glimpse of myself in the mirror. And I don't think I've done all that bad for a girl whose mama never lets her wear makeup. Obviously, Danielle feels differently. She scrubs off my eye shadow too.

Mama won't let me wear a lick of makeup, not even lip gloss. She says twelve is too young to be thinking about stuff like that. It'll only draw attention from the wrong people. She really means boys.

So that's why every morning I meet Danielle in the restroom before the bell rings and put on some of her makeup. Unfortunately, Danielle's *second* best friend A. J. meets us here too.

And since Danielle is giving me a movie-star makeover, A. J. (who hates being ignored) has to throw in her two cents. So she smiles a mean smile and says,

"She was probably off somewhere looking for a doughnut. And by the time she looked up, God had run out of the good lip-making material and had to use a bunch of leftovers for hers."

That girl can say some really foolish things. So I say something foolish right back to her, "I see you were doing the same thing when he was giving out cute faces."

But before I can pat myself on the back for roasting her, A. J. plants her hands on her skinny little hips and says, "Looks like you came around twice though when he was giving out chins."

Then she just cracks up, like her jokes are so funny.

"Whatever," I say. I think about checking her again about her ugly face. But she already knows I hate being plump way more than she hates being ugly, even if she does look like a twenty-year-old bulldog.

"There," Danielle says, turning me to face the mirror. "Perfect."

"Wow," I whisper.

"You mean, 'Woe'," A. J. says, making an ugly (I mean, uglier) face at me in the mirror.

I make one back. And hope she chokes on Pine-Sol too.

"You look good, Jimmy Lee," Danielle assures me.

A. J. grunts then leans back and gives me that look again. She crosses her arms over her chest and says, "Maybe if she got some of that fat sucked off them cheeks and them big ol' lips she'd look good."

Then she cracks up again, slapping her leg and everything. And it doesn't even bother her that she's the only one laughing.

Danielle cuts her eyes at her.

"What?" A. J. says, acting all innocent.

"Stop hatin'," Danielle says.

A. J. frowns and slings her backpack over her shoulder. She stomps toward the door and yanks it open then turns and looks me up and down again. "What's there to hate?" she says.

"Whatever," I call after her, even though she's already disappeared into the noise of the crowded hallway.

Angry tears sting my eyes, and I quickly turn my head before Danielle sees them.

But she already knows what's up. So she goes fishing through that junky purse of hers for a tissue. "Girl, you better not start crying." She hands me a pink tissue that looks used. "You know that mascara ain't waterproof."

I take the tissue and grit my teeth to keep from crying. I carefully dab my eyes and fight back a sniffle. "I can't stand her," I say.

"She's just jealous," Danielle says.

"Jealous of what?" I step back to give her a good look at the roll wrapped around my waist.

Danielle grins. "Yeah, but look at that face."

We both laugh for a second until Danielle gets all serious and starts rearranging the contents of her bulky purse.

"A. J. acts like I'm not supposed to have any friends but her," she says, leaning toward the mirror to check her makeup one last time before we head to class.

"You mean she doesn't want you to have *me* as a friend," I say.

Danielle turns up her nose. And I can't tell if it's because of the Pine-Sol, or because of what I just said. She knows A. J. has been snubbing me since the first day of middle school—the day she saw the name **Jimmy Lee Easton** on the class roster and thought I was a boy. She's still mad at me for embarrassing herself about how cute she thought I'd be, only to find out I was a girl.

"Jimmy. Now that's a name you don't see every day," she'd said, running her finger over my name in a way that had given me goose bumps.

She lingered over my name for a second then said, "I bet he's cute though."

I was standing right behind her, so I laughed and said, "I'm not a he. I'm a she."

She whipped around and stared at me like I had barfed up my breakfast. She observed me from head to toe then said, "That's a stupid name for a girl."

But Danielle turned to me with a broad smile and said, "Hi. I'm Danielle. Nice to meet you, Jimmy."

I smiled back and said, "Most folks call me Jimmy Lee, but you can call me Jimmy if you want."

"Jimmy Lee," Danielle said sweetly. "That's unique."

I shrugged and said, "I'm named after my daddy."

A. J. snorted. "What kind of fool would name a girl Jimmy Lee?"

"My mama's not a fool," I said. "And I'm proud of my name."

Danielle smiled and said, "I like your name. It's cool."

"It's stupid," A. J. said. Then she turned up her nose and stomped away. She hasn't stopped torturing me since. It's not like *her* name is all that great. It's Allelujah Joy, which is why she wants everybody to call her A. J.

Danielle snaps her purse closed and says, "Let's get out of here, girl. You know Mr. Davis wasn't kidding yesterday when he said: 'If you're late, count on staying with Mrs. Conley in the detention room for the day.'"

"You know I don't wanna miss this field trip." I grab my backpack from the counter. "Thanks to Mr. Davis's no-mama-chaperoned-field-trip rule, I don't have to worry about Darlynn Easton tagging along, breathing down my neck."

Danielle laughs. "Why do you always call your mama by her whole name like that?"

"'Cause that's what she calls herself."

I drop my backpack on the counter again and pose in front of the mirror. "'Darlynn Easton don't take no stuff off nobody'," I say, mimicking my wanna-be-tough mama. "Mess with me, and you'll find that your mouth just wrote a check that your behind can't cash."

Danielle shakes her head. "Your mama's so cool."

"Cool? Please. She's annoying."

"At least she wants to spend time with you."

"No. She wants to keep an eye on me," I say. "Now, your mama's cool. She lets you do whatever you want."

"Yeah," Danielle says, rolling her eyes. "*Such* a great mom."

She frowns and gets quiet for a minute. Then she suddenly beams, "Hey! At least we can finally sit together on the bus."

"Yeah, if A. J. doesn't try to knock me off the seat," I say, throwing my backpack over my shoulder.

Danielle stops at the door and gives me a reassuring smile. "It's gonna be a great day, Jimmy Lee. Don't let A. J. spoil it."

I half smile and mumble, "That's gonna be kinda hard, unless you put a bag over that ugly face of hers."

"Seriously, Jimmy Lee," Danielle says. "Don't let her bully you like that."

I stop and think about the field trip. A field trip without Mama. And my spirits suddenly soar. "You're right," I say. "Today *is* gonna be a great day. And there's no way I'm letting A. J. or Darlynn Easton or anybody else ruin it for me."

All the World's a Stage

*"All the world's a stage, and all the men and
women merely players."*
~ As You Like It

A.J. McCracken. Darlynn Easton. Gloria Jean Aberdeen. I didn't count on that last one. The school secretary. As soon as we settle into class, her voice crackles on the intercom. "Mr. Davis?"

"Yes, Mrs. Aberdeen?" Mr. Davis replies.

"Can you send Jimmy Easton to the office? His mother is here to see him."

Mr. Davis frowns and says, "*Her.*"

"Excuse me?" says Mrs. Aberdeen.

"Jimmy Lee is a *her*," says Mr. Davis.

"What's that again?" Mrs. Aberdeen asks, over the *snap, crackle, pop* of the intercom.

Mr. Davis shakes his head and motions me toward the door. "She's on her way," he calls up to the intercom.

I shoot a look at Danielle. Her face looks as panicked as mine. She pulls another slightly used tissue from her purse (this one's light blue) and holds it out for me to grab on my way out the door.

A. J. snickers.

Now I really feel like crying. I wasted my morning inhaling Pine-Sol for nothing. I quickly wipe off my eye shadow and lip gloss when I get into the hallway then stuff the tissue into my jeans pocket.

Why was Mama at the school anyway? What could she possibly want? Mr. Davis had sent home a note saying that parents couldn't attend the field trip. Plus, I had reminded her of it a thousand times.

Maybe something had happened to Aunt Millie. Like a heart attack. Yeah, right. Like I should be so lucky.

When I step into the office, Mrs. Aberdeen's mouth flies open like that's the first time she's ever seen me. "You're—a girl," she stammers.

I nod. "Yes, ma'am. I'm a girl." We have this I'm-a-girl intro every time I come to the office. We've had it six times this year already.

Mrs. Aberdeen tilts her glasses down and stares at me without her bifocals. She squints and says, "Oh, yeah. Now I remember."

Mama's standing by Mrs. Aberdeen's spotless desk. And I swear she's trying to embarrass me to death, wearing her Pizza Hut uniform. It's barely 8:30. She doesn't have to be at work until 10.

She knows I hate that uniform. And it's not just because it always smells like onions and green peppers, either. It's because it makes her look skinnier than she already is.

Aunt Millie says I sucked all the fat from her when I was born. I hope she doesn't think that's some kind of compliment.

"Hey, Mama," I say, glancing at her suspiciously. "What's up?"

Mama reaches into her pocket and pulls out a bunch of one-dollar bills. They're all crumpled. "I forgot to give you money this morning," she says, holding the bills toward me.

I stare at her hand like she's holding a rattlesnake. "I don't need any money. I told you everything was paid for when I turned in the money with the permission slip."

"Well, take it anyway." She grabs my hand and presses the bills into it.

I push the money back into her hand. "But I don't need it."

"What if you wanna buy something?"

Now I'm really annoyed. Mr. Davis's note specifically said not to bring spending money. Mama posted the note on the dresser mirror, so I know she read it every day.

I know why she's here, and I'm not falling for it.

"I can't take any money," I say stiffly.

Mama doesn't budge. She's been on every field trip I've taken since kindergarten, scared to death to let me out of her sight, except for school—I guess because she keeps losing people like my grandma and my daddy. And by losing them, I mean they died, not that they got lost somewhere like in the woods or the jungle or the mall.

Mama tries to hand me the money again, and I shake my head. "Mr. Davis doesn't want us bringing money, Mama."

She doesn't say anything. She already knows this.

I shrug and think, *Go away, please. You're not going on this field trip.* But instead, I force a smile and say, "You know how Mr. Davis is. Some kids might not have money, and he doesn't want anybody feeling left out."

I keep smiling, hoping she'll put her crumpled money away and leave. *Please don't pick a fight with Mr. Davis and embarrass me to death.*

But she doesn't. She just stares at me with sad eyes.

I've fallen for the sad eyes before. And regretted it. But not today. I can't let her ruin this field trip.

We stand there staring at each other until Mrs. Aberdeen breaks the silence. "Well, shoot! If y'all don't want the money, I'll take it." She sticks out her bejeweled hand.

Mama glances at her and fakes a smile. She stuffs the bills back into her pocket and turns to me. "You have fun. Okay, baby?" But her eyes are saying, *Don't go. Please, don't go.* She tried that this morning, but Aunt Millie, surprisingly, had yelled at her and said, "Let the child be, Darlynn."

Mama leans over and kisses me on the cheek, and I almost gag at the scent of coffee and cigarettes. To make matters worse, Mrs. Aberdeen stares at us like we're a stage play.

I wish I had the super power to disappear. Or at least hide behind the curtain.

Instead, I turn and hurry out of the office. I don't bother saying goodbye to Mama. I just leave her standing there with her stinky Pizza Hut uniform and her pocketful of crumpled one-dollar bills.

You Too, Danielle?

"Et tu, Brute?"
~ Julius Caesar

Everybody is all super hyped because Mr. I-can-drive-a-school-bus-and-drink-a-RedBull-and-talk-on-my-cell-phone-at-the-same-time Gibbons, a.k.a. Mr. Joyride, is our driver today. But Mama would have a fit if she knew, especially since we're going on the interstate. She swore she was gonna get Mr. Gibbons fired the last time he drove us to a field trip.

But lucky for me, Mama doesn't know. Or I'd be at home with pinched-face Aunt Millie right now, trying to ignore the sound of old-time gospel music blaring from her fifty-year-old radio. And today's Friday, the thirteenth, too? I'm surprised either one of them let me out of the house.

So instead of listening to "When the Saints Go Marching In" for the umpteenth time, I'm listening to music on Danielle's phone. And Mama would kill me if she knew that too, seeing that Danielle's mama lets her listen to all the cool music. A reggae song about a man being gunned down and left for dead is playing right now, and my eyes are tearing up. Every time I hear that song I think about my daddy. He died right before I was born. Mama says some fool shot him for no good reason then just ran off and let him die.

But Aunt Millie says Mama's lying.

Every time I bring it up, she says, "Child, that boy ain't dead. Your mama just tells herself that lie because that boy ran off and left her. He ran off right before you were born."

But Mama says Aunt Millie is the liar. And I believe Mama. Because if my daddy was alive, I know he'd come see me.

"Yo, Jimmy!" A. J. yells from the front of the bus.

I snatch out the earbuds and glare at her. "What?"

A. J. thumbs toward the side of the bus, where Mr. Davis and Ms. Randell are checking their class lists. "Mr. Davis wants to see you."

"What for?"

A. J. shrugs. "How should I know?"

I hand Danielle her phone and ask her to save my seat.

I head toward the front of the bus as A. J. heads toward the back. She politely moves to the side and lets me pass. And as soon as I do, she heads for my seat.

She looks back at me and sneers. "You're so green."

She plops right in my spot beside Danielle. And Danielle doesn't even say a word. She just hands A. J. her phone like I wasn't even using it.

I stare out the window and see Mr. Davis and Ms. Randell engaged in conversation. I don't waste my time or theirs, because I know Mr. Davis didn't call for me.

I glance around the bus. All the seats are taken, except Mr. Davis's, Ms. Randell's, and one other. My stomach knots at the sight of it.

I take a deep breath, stroll over, and plop down on the seat behind Mr. Joyride—right beside Leonard George, a grungy boy who always smells like poop.

Something's Rotten

"Something is rotten in the state of Denmark."
~ Hamlet

No matter how hard I try to pretend I'm sleeping, Leonard George won't stop talking. And everything about him smells like poop, especially his breath. It's horrible, like something's crawled inside of him, forgot to come out, then died and rotted.

"What school did you go to?" he asks.

"Danforth," I say with my eyes still closed, wishing I could close my nose too.

"Me too!" he beams.

I don't respond. I couldn't care less where he went to school. Now if it were Danielle, *that* would be another story.

See, kids come to our school, Clark-Cooke Middle, from three different elementary schools. Clark

Elementary is the one in the nice neighborhood with fenced yards and attached garages, where the daddies go off to work every day and the mamas "stay home" and volunteer at the school every day.

Clark is Danielle's old school.

Cooke Elementary is the school in a neighborhood almost as nice as Clark's, except the mamas don't get to stay home and volunteer. They have to go to work just like the daddies.

Cooke is A. J.'s old school.

Then there's Danforth, my old school. And, obviously, Poop Boy's too. It's named after some old guy, Willard Danforth, who supposedly did some spectacular deed for the city a long time ago. Danforth Elementary sits in the middle of government housing projects, where hardly anybody goes to work every day. And the daddies sometimes don't even bother to come home.

Clark and Cooke neighborhoods are right next to each other. But Danforth isn't. We're separated by a railroad track. Literally.

And since Clark and Cooke are close together, Danielle and A. J. get to go to the same church. That's why they've known each other since forever.

I, on the other hand, attend Aunt Millie's long-skirt-no-makeup-wearing church—Church of the Most Holiest—on the other side of town. Hence, my lack of cool friends.

"How come I never saw you at Danforth?" Poop Boy asks.

Eyes still closed, head resting on the back of the seat, feet wanting to walk to the back of the bus, hand wanting to slap A. J. across her ugly face, I mutter, "Maybe because I wasn't looking for you."

Poop Boy ignores my insult and keeps yapping. "You live in Harvey Estates?"

I open my eyes and glare at him, wondering for the hundredth time why anybody would call a government housing project "Estates." They're two-bedroom duplexes, for goodness sake.

"Yes," I answer, dryly.

"Me too!" Poop Boy beams.

Who cares? I turn my head toward the aisle. *Why do flies love that scent?*

"How come your name is Jimmy Lee?" Poop Boy asks.

I keep my face turned toward the aisle. I shrug.

"Well, how come?" he asks again.

-22-

I turn and frown at him. "It was my daddy's name," I say, trying to hold my breath and talk at the same time.

"Wow. That's so cool. I'm named after my pop too. But I'm a boy, so it's not a big deal like with you."

"It's not a big deal," I mumble.

"But it's so cool. So *cool*," he says, breathing out poop scent.

Too bad it's late spring, and it's too hot for a jacket. If I had one, I could at least cover my face.

Poop Boy squirms in his seat. And I want to gag. What I wouldn't give for a bottle of Ms. Wicker's Pine-Sol right now. I'd drown him in it.

"You ever been to the Civil Rights Museum?" he asks.

I shake my head from side to side. I'm barely breathing. And the bumping bus doesn't help one bit either.

"I have," Poop Boy says proudly. "My pop took me."

I. Don't. Care.

"That's why I always sit at the front of the bus."

I cut my eyes at him. "You sit at the front of the bus because your daddy took you to the Civil Rights Museum?"

Poop Boy laughs. His teeth are really yellow. He shakes his head. "No. I sit on the front seat because of Rosa Parks and the sacrifice she made."

Okay. Now he's trying to make me feel ignorant. "Whatever," I say, trying to sound as snarky as possible and hold my breath at the same time.

"No. Really," Poop Boy says. "Pop said we should honor the people who worked so hard for our freedom."

His face is as serious as a heart attack. I clear my throat to keep from laughing. I can't believe his pop teaches him about the civil rights movement but not about proper hygiene.

"You can hang out with me at the museum if you want," he offers. "I could tell you all the stuff my pop told me."

I cringe. "Um, no thanks," I mutter.

Poop Boy turns around and stares toward the back of the bus. "Guess you wanna hang out with your friends, huh?"

I shrug uncaringly. "I guess I do."

Poop Boy drops his eyes to his ashy hands and starts picking dirt from his nails.

I close my eyes again and try to ignore him and his funky odor. I don't have time for his problems. I have enough of my own.

To Sleep

"To sleep, perchance to dream-ay, there's the rub."
~ Hamlet

I really want to fall asleep, but now Mr. Joyride's cell phone is ringing.

He checks the rearview mirror to see if Mr. Davis is looking, then he answers his phone. Ms. Randell is sitting right across from me, reading *People* magazine. But I guess her opinion doesn't count.

"Yeah, 'sup," Mr. Gibbons says into the phone. "Nah, I ain't busy. Just taking some kids downtown to a field trip."

He wedges the phone between his ear and shoulder and takes a gulp of Red Bull. I shake my head. He could at least use Bluetooth or something.

"Yeah, I'll be there tonight. No problem," Mr. No-Hands-Free says. He takes another gulp of Red Bull, puts it down then checks the rearview mirror. He barely misses a truck in front of us as he quickly switches to the left lane.

A bunch of kids raise their hands and scream, like we're at an amusement park. I'm so glad Mama's not here. The last field trip took us on a winding road. And, boy, did Mr. Gibbons have fun with that.

He zooms past the 18-wheeler then zips back into the right lane. Since we're going downhill, he makes the bus zigzag.

Kids scream again.

Poop Boy is about to freak out.

I'm cracking up inside.

Bet you'll move to the back of the bus now, Mr. Black History.

Mr. Gibbons is getting a kick out of making the kids scream, so he brakes and the bus jerks forward.

"Gibbons!" Mr. Davis yells from the middle of the bus.

"Ah, be quiet, Mr. Davis. We're having fun," that annoying, but oh-so-good-looking, Carlos Trujillo, yells from the back.

"It's not too late to cancel," Mr. Davis yells back.

"Chill, Mr. Davis, you ain't no cop," Carlos says. And everybody laughs. Except Poop Boy.

"Gibbons!" Mr. Davis yells again. "Drive this bus correctly or get off at the next exit and take us back to the school."

Mr. Gibbons raises his cell-phone-free hand, salutes Mr. Davis and says, "Aye-aye, Cap'n." Then he floors the bus one last time before he starts driving normal again.

Carlos says something in Spanish, and we all laugh. (We have no idea what he said.)

"Trujillo," Mr. Davis says. "Don't let that snarky attitude ruin this field trip for the rest of the students. I'll have Mr. Gibbons turn this bus around faster than you can blink."

Make him move to the front, Mr. Davis. And make Poop Boy move to the back, I silently plead.

"Ah, c'mon, Mr. Davis. It's all good," Carlos says.

Mr. Davis says something in Spanish, and Carlos falls as silent as a stick.

The kids in the back start complaining to Mr. Davis about what he said, even though they have no clue what it was. He threatens to cancel the field trip again, and everybody groans.

Everybody except Poop Boy. His eyes are tearing up. He acts just like my mama.

We're about five minutes from the downtown exit, so I close my eyes again. I try to hold my breath, too, but it's not working.

I just want to have a relaxing day at the museum and forget about Mama and all her worrying. Forget about Aunt Millie and all her righteousness. And forget about A. J. and her ugly bulldog face.

But as soon as I relax my eyelids, I hear Will Smith "gettin' jiggy wit it" again. I open my eyes just in time to see Mr. Gibbons answer his phone and check the rearview mirror at the same time.

"Mr. Gibbons!" I scream. "Watch out!"

The bright red lights on the big truck in front of us are flashing wildly. And the bus is approaching them quickly.

My fingers grip the seat. "Mr. Gibbons!" I yell.

When Mr. Gibbons drops his cell phone and throws both hands on the steering wheel, all I can do is squeeze my eyes shut and scream.

Everybody else on the front of the bus screams too.

The rest of the bus joins in, thinking it's another joyride.

"Gibbons!" Mr. Davis yells.

Mr. Gibbons slams hard on the brakes. But he's too late.

The sound of screeching brakes fills the air. Then BOOM!

Before I can brace myself, my body flies forward and slams into the front panel of the bus. Pain cuts through my head like a giant knife and doesn't stop until it reaches my neck. It goes straight down my spine and into my legs.

Warm blood trickles down my face.

The scent of burning rubber and gas fills my nostrils.

Blood fills my mouth.

I choke.

My body numbs.

My vision blurs.

My eyelids drop.

I finally fall asleep.

The Lady Doth Protest
Too Much

"The lady doth protest too much, methinks."
~ **Hamlet**

Ever since I was a little kid, like three or four, I've been a dreamer. Mama says so. And I don't mean a dreamer as in someone who has high hopes for the future, I mean a dreamer as in I have dreams that feel like they're really happening.

Mama says I would wake up in the middle of the night screaming my head off. She'd say, "Go back to sleep, Jimmy Lee. You're having a bad dream."

Now what kind of sense did that make? Especially to a little kid? Why would I want to go back to something that was scaring the stink out of me?

Sometimes I would dream about the same places over and over again. Places that don't exist in real life, only in my dreams. But they're *my* places. My rooms. My houses. My buildings. My streets. My cities. My people. Over and over again. Sometimes they were scary. Sometimes not.

But this dream is different. This dream is one of those really real ones. And it's in a real place. Harvey Estates. I know because I see the square brick units that make up each set of two-bedroom duplexes. Look-alike duplexes with green front doors. And a big living room window to the right of the door. And a smaller bedroom window to the left. With green shutters to match the green doors.

And there's our unit. Number 22. The number is the only thing that makes them different. The number on the outside. And the people on the inside. Otherwise, everything in Harvey Estates looks just alike. Mama says it's a government conspiracy.

And speaking of Mama, there she is, in her Pizza Hut uniform. She's standing on the side of our unit. Well, she's leaning against the wall, actually—with a cigarette dangling from her lips. She smokes like thirty of 'em a day.

Aunt Millie says they're gonna kill her.

But Mama says, "We all gotta die from something."

Then Aunt Millie says, "If I had a choice, it wouldn't be lung cancer."

For once, I agree with Aunt Millie.

I can tell Mama's angry, even in a dream. And I know who she's angry at...Mr. Davis.

"Mr. No-Parents-Allowed Davis," I hear her muttering between puffs on her cigarette. "Mr. Give-Your-Kids-Some-Space-And-Let-Them-Grow-Up Davis."

She takes one last puff then throws the cigarette butt to the ground. She crushes the life out of it, spits, then says, "He just ruined my day."

I've got to test the waters. I stand right next to her and yell, "Mama!"

She doesn't hear me. I like this dream.

Mama shakes the pack to release another cigarette. Even in a dream, she smokes non-stop. She's been smoking since she was seventeen.

Virginia Slims.

"You've come a long way, baby," as she likes to say.

I guess she's right. Because now she's twenty-nine, and the habit's too hard to break.

Oh, this *is* a good dream, because here comes Ms. Shirley, the neighborhood beauty queen, who's always dressed up with nowhere to go. People say she's as old as Aunt Millie. But I know they're lying. There's no way a woman as old as Aunt Millie could walk like that in three-inch heels.

This dream is too real. Ms. Shirley's actually wearing her fancy "spring green" Ann Klein suit she bought from Goodwill for eight dollars. And she's wearing her blonde wig (which is such a contrast from her dark brown complexion). She looks exactly the same as when I saw her on my way to school this morning!

"Mornin', Darlynn," she approaches Mama and says. I never noticed that her voice is all crackly like the school intercom. Maybe she is as old as Aunt Millie.

Mama blows a smoke ring. "Hey, Ms. Shirley," she says.

Mama offers the cigarette pack to Ms. Shirley. She takes it and shakes one out for herself. They're both gonna die.

Ms. Shirley raises her hand to her eyes to block out the early morning sun. "You back at Pizza Hut?" she asks, squinting, the cigarette wedged between her lips.

Mama shakes her head. "Nah," she says, smoothing down the front of her onion and bell pepper scented uniform. "Just need to keep the Old Mill happy."

The Old Mill is Aunt Millie. And Mama obviously has lost another job and is pretending she hasn't. Aunt Millie says we're not pulling our weight. I guess she's right.

"So, what you gonna do?" Ms. Shirley asks.

Mama shrugs, places the cigarette between her lips then sucks in her cheeks real hard. She holds them there for a second. A long second.

She finally takes the cigarette out, blows out a foot-long stream of smoke, and sighs. "I'll find something," she says. "Darlynn Easton always does."

Ms. Shirley nods. "Sure you will, honey."

Then they're both silent for a moment.

Ms. Shirley only smokes half her cigarette then snuffs out its remains with one of her spiky pink heels. Mama scowls at her.

Ms. Shirley turns from Mama's stare and looks toward the six-foot tall wood fence that separates Harvey Estates from the rest of the world. "I hear Domino's is hiring," she says.

Mama turns up her nose. "I'd never work for the competition."

This time, Ms. Shirley shrugs and changes the subject. "Jimmy go on that field trip this morning?" she asks. (I don't know why she always calls me Jimmy instead of Jimmy Lee.)

Mama throws back her head and starts laughing like she's lost her mind.

Ms. Shirley laughs too.

"Hey, what's so funny?" I yell. But they don't hear me.

Then the dream gets really weird...because now I'm in the kitchen with Aunt Millie!

And it smells *sooo* good in here. Aunt Millie's making pies for the bake sale at the church tomorrow. I can see that peach cobbler through the window on the door of the oven. The juice is bubbling up out of the crust.

My mouth waters.

Looks like Aunt Millie has outdone herself this time.

Now if she would just turn off that fifty-year-old radio, this dream would be perfect.

And Aunt Millie's singing right along while she stands at the counter and rolls out dough for another pie crust.

I stand right beside her and cross my arms. "Give it up, Aunt Millie," I say. "There's a reason Pastor Lewis asked you to bake pies instead of lead the choir."

I'm loving this dream. It's so different from any I've ever had. I've never been able to watch people and talk to them without being seen or heard. Well, except that time I watched myself beat up Aunt Millie in a dream. Now that was cool.

I make faces at Aunt Millie then stick my tongue out and sing, "Ms. Millie, Ms. Millie, as mean as a Billy. You think you're so smart, but you're just silly."

I used to sing that song when I was six. A girl named Felicia taught me. She once lived in the unit attached to ours.

Aunt Millie called Felicia's mama a harlot. Felicia was only eight at the time, but she already knew what the word meant. After she told me, we made up the song.

Aunt Millie's nose is twitching like she can smell me or something. I know it's only a dream, but I step away from her anyway. Then the dream changes scenes again.

Now I'm in our bedroom with Mama. Mama's lying on our bed. If this wasn't a dream, I'd be wondering how she got in here without Aunt Millie hearing her. But knowing Mama, she could do it. She's sneaky like that. Aunt Millie says Mama's ability to sneak in and out of the apartment without her knowing is how I came about.

Okay, now I know I'm dreaming. Darlynn Easton's reading a book!

Mama doesn't read anything but the captions on the movies that she doesn't want Aunt Millie to hear her watching.

I peek over at the cover *Transforming Your Life: The Power of Prayer*. Interesting title. Especially seeing that Mama claims she doesn't believe in God. I wonder who (or what) she's planning on praying to.

Wait. This is a dream. Never mind. Anything is possible.

Good grits and gravy! Mama just threw the book across the room and jumped off the bed.

What is going on here? She's breaking out of this room like the place is on fire.

"Aunt Millie! Aunt Millieeee!" she's yelling, her voice high-screeched.

(See, this is why kids wake up screaming in the middle of the night.)

Okay. Now I'm back in the kitchen. ...sometimes I hate dreams.

Aunt Millie's eyes are bugged bigger than golf balls. Mama's scared the living daylights out of her.

"Darlynn?" Her voice startles. "What're you doing here? How—oh, never mind," Aunt Millie says, shaking the shock from her head. (Her hands never leave that pie crust.)

"What's all that noise for?" she asks Mama.

Oh no. Tears are streaming down Mama's face. I don't like this dream anymore. Something bad is about to happen.

"It's Jimmy Lee!" Mama says, gasping for air.

"What's me?" I yell. But they can't hear me.

My throat tightens, and my head starts to spin.

I really don't like this dream anymore. I want to wake up. I pinch my arm. "Wake up!" I yell.

But, I don't.

Something Wicked

"Something wicked this way comes."
~ Macbeth

I'm in tears because my arm is bruised, and I'm still in this horrible dream. Aunt Millie's on the phone now, looking petrified. And Mama's crying and howling like somebody died. This is one of those dreams where I know something bad is about to happen, like something wicked is gonna show up any minute. And I'm not gonna wake up in time to escape it.

"Mama!" I yell, but she can't hear me. She can't even see me!

I try Aunt Millie. "Aunt Millie! Please! Hear me! See me! Smell me! Anything!"

But her face doesn't change. No nose-twitching. Nothing. She's just standing there with the phone to her ear, her face ashen.

Then the room goes black, and I wait for the monster to show up.

But it doesn't. Instead I'm in the back seat of Ms. Shirley's hundred-year-old Cadillac that she calls Lil' Shirl. And Lil' Shirl is flying over speed bumps like they don't exist.

Mama's in the front seat with Ms. Shirley, and Aunt Millie's in the back. Smack dab in the middle, like I'm not even here!

And as fast as this dream put us in this car, it takes us to the hospital.

Please let me wake up. This can't be good.

Lil' Shirl stops so fast that she sends everybody flying forward. (Hundred-year-old cars don't have seatbelts.)

Mama gets out before Ms. Shirley turns off the engine.

Everything goes black again, and all I hear are swishing noises. Everything around me is so dark that I can feel it, like a big black blanket. And the swishing. Like a swing. On a playground. Swish. Swing forward. Swish. Swing back.

I call for Mama again, and I don't even hear my own voice this time. Just the swing. Swish. Swish. Swish.

Then oomph! I'm knocked over. Like somebody kicked me.

Then everything brightens again, like a light just came on. And I'm on the playground at my old school, Danforth Elementary. And I've just been kicked over by a girl on a swing.

She comes at me again, and I see her face. It's uglier than a cricket's.

It's A.J. And she didn't even go to my old school!

I see another girl pushing A.J.'s swing.

Danielle.

And they're both laughing.

"Wake up!" I yell at myself. And A.J. kicks me again.

I cower and cover my face.

"Hey! Leave my girlfriend alone!" someone yells.

I look up.

It's Poop Boy. He smiles at me and blows me a kiss.

"Somebody please wake me up!" I scream.

Still Dreaming?

*"We are such stuff as dreams are made on; and our
little life is rounded with a sleep."*
~ **The Tempest**

A soft breeze brushes my face, finally stirring me
from my sleep. But I can't open my eyes. I try, but they
feel like they're glued shut. And no matter how much I
strain, they won't open.

I try to open my mouth to cry for help. But that
doesn't work either. My lips won't move. I don't know
how long I've been sleeping, but I know some time has
passed. My body is stiff, like I've been sleeping for days.

And I know I'm not on the bus anymore either.
I'm outside, and I'm lying on something hard. Not the
ground, but up higher, like a bench. I think.

The sun is warm on my face, despite the breeze. And a bird is flapping right by my head, chirping near my ear. A bird! Right by my head!

I smell flowers, too, and spices, like Aunt Millie's peach cobbler. I remember the dream now. That wild dream with Mama and Ms. Shirley. And Aunt Millie and her singing. And the peach cobbler. And riding in Lil' Shirl to the hospital. And A.J. and Danielle on the playground. And Poop Boy. Oh my gosh, Poop Boy— who blew me a poopy-breath kiss!

I think I'm in a park. At least that's what it sounds like. But how did I get here? When the bus crashed, I must've been thrown from it and landed in a park. But does anybody know I'm here?

"Help!" I try to cry out. But all I do is moan.

Okay. This is a bad dream. I know it is. I've had these before. Dreams where I know I'm dreaming and I try to wake up. But I can't.

That's what this is. A bad dream. I'm still having bad dreams. That's why I smell peach cobbler. Aunt Millie's already baking her pies for whatever that thing is they're having at church on Saturday.

Is today Saturday? Did I miss the field trip? No. I remember the bus. Or was that a dream, too?

I've gotta wake up.

I shake myself, or try to anyway. That usually works.

But not this time.

"Wake up!" I yell at myself.

Nothing.

"Jimmy Lee," a woman's voice whispers.

I jump.

That wasn't Mama. She would've yelled, "Get up, Jimmy Lee Easton! RISE and shine! And SHINE and rise!"

And it certainly wasn't Aunt Millie. She never sets foot in our room.

So maybe I'm not dreaming. "Ms. Randell?" I try to say.

I moan instead.

I try to open my eyes again, but I can't. And straining them takes so much effort.

The woman touches my shoulder. I flinch.

"Jimmy Lee," she says. "It's time to wake up."

Wake up? What do you think I'm trying to do, lady?

I moan again, aching to say something.

"I want to go home," I try to say. But nothing comes out.

The woman rubs my shoulder. "It's okay, Jimmy Lee," she whispers. "You're safe now."

I stiffen. That's not Ms. Randell.

Who is this woman? And what does she mean *safe now*? Did she call an ambulance?

Wait. I don't feel that stabbing pain in my head anymore.

I remember the blood. I raise my hand to my face. But I don't feel anything. This woman, whoever she is, must've cleaned it off.

"I'm not hurt anymore," I try to tell her. "The pain is gone. The blood is gone. Please call my mama."

But my thoughts only come out as moans. And this woman has no idea that I'm okay. She probably thinks I'm some little kid who fell asleep at the park and got left behind. But wait. She knows my name. And she saw the blood on my face. She knows I've been hurt. And she knows who I am!

A glob of wetness suddenly hits my face, right on my eyelid. Another glob hits the other eyelid. A thick liquid rolls off the sides of my face.

I wipe it off and blink. And my eyes finally open.

This isn't a dream. I *am* in a park. And, I'm lying on a bench.

I look up and see a bird hovering over me. Right over my head.

I feel my eyelids, and they're both wet. Did that bird just *poop* on my eyes?

I sit up and look around. Flowers of all kinds and colors surround the bench. And the only sound I hear is chirping birds and water, like a waterfall, somewhere in the distance. This isn't a park. It's more like a garden. Yeah, that's it. It's the botanic gardens. And that has to be a fake waterfall I hear.

But how did I get here?

The last thing I remember is seeing those bright red brake lights on that truck.

Where is everybody? Where's the bus? The accident? How the heck did I get here?

I try to look around, but my eyes fall on this woman who is standing in front of me. She is the most beautiful person I've ever seen in my life, and I can't stop staring at her.

"Well, hello there," she says. And I startle. Her voice is sultry and smooth, like in an old TV show.

But that face. So beautiful.

Her skin is like copper, like a shiny new penny. And it's as smooth as her voice. Every feature on her face is sized just right. No big nose. No too-thick lips.

No fuzzy, double eyebrows. As perfect as a photoshopped model.

And that hair. So long. So thick. So black. So shiny…flowing in waves around her face.

But why is she so dressed up in a garden? Her dress is like the silkiest, reddest, most brilliant dress I've ever seen. With sparkling sequins all around the neckline and down the sleeves, like an evening gown for a fancy party. She even has a little red heart-shaped purse hanging from her wrist.

I guess the shock in my face amuses her. "You've just about slept the day away," she says, laughing, her eyes sparkling brighter than the sequins on her dress.

Slept the day away? What does she mean *slept the day away?* How long have I been out here, and *why* am I out here?

"Oh, Jimmy Lee, you're so beautiful!" she says, touching my cheek.

I flinch. I open my mouth to speak, but nothing comes out.

"Oh, your voice," she says. "You lost your voice during the transition."

Transition? What *transition?* Where has this woman taken me?

"Help!" I try to scream. But I moan instead.

"There, there," she says, reaching out for me. "Calm down."

I lean back onto the bench, moaning, "No! Get away from me!"

The woman takes a step back and whispers, "Oh, dear, I've frightened you."

She motions for the bird. The one that's been hanging around ever since I regained consciousness. She holds out her hand, and the bird poops on it. Then she takes that same nasty hand and reaches for my throat.

"No!" I try to scream and throw my hands up.

The woman sighs. "Looks like I'm going to need some help."

She whistles. It's the loveliest sound I've ever heard in my life. But I don't take my hands away from my throat. Then I realize that isn't why she's whistling, because out of nowhere, three more birds show up.

They're not very big birds. Just the average bird you'd find perched in the average tree. But suddenly all four of them attack me, grabbing my arms, pulling them away from my throat. And no matter how much I struggle, I'm no match for these four birds.

While the birds hold my arms back, the woman quickly lunges for my throat with her bird-poop hand. She puts her hand on my throat.

I try to scream, but the warmth of her hand soothes me. My throat tingles.

The woman steps back and smiles. "There," she says. "Now say something."

I swallow then open my mouth. "Hello," I whisper, and my voice sounds strange.

Then all of a sudden, I want to cry, because I don't know where I am.

Where's the bus? And my class? And Mr. Davis? And Danielle?

Where's my mama?

I burst into tears.

The woman sits beside me and puts her arm around my shoulders and says, "There, there, let it out, darlin'. It's okay. Just let it out."

Tears flow down my face, and my shoulders shake, despite the comfort of the woman's touch. Because now, I do know what this is, but I don't want to accept it. I'm in a garden—the most beautiful garden I've ever seen in my life—more beautiful than any picture I've ever seen. The whole place is peaceful and smells like flowers and spices. Strange, *strong* birds fly around and poop on people on purpose.

Even the sky is a perfect blue.

One minute I'm on a bus ride to a field trip. An accident happens. I hit my head. Now the pain is gone, and I'm in a garden with a woman I've never seen before—a woman who knows my name. I cry harder, because I just can't believe this has happened to me. I'm only twelve years old. I'm just a kid. This can't be right. I can't be *dead*.

Good or Bad?

"There is nothing either good or bad, but thinking makes it so."
~ Hamlet

"Mama's gonna be *sooo* mad at me," I say between sobs. "She told me not to go on that field trip."

The woman in the red dress hands me a red satin handkerchief. "Your mother had no idea of knowing what would happen today, my dear," she says.

I have no idea where she got the handkerchief from either, because I never saw her open that little heart-shaped purse. But I take the handkerchief and wipe my face and blow my nose anyway. I can't believe I have real tears and snot. But I guess if a bird can poop, then I should be able to cry.

I hand the woman her handkerchief back, feeling bad that I've ruined it. But she only smiles. She takes the handkerchief, holds it out, and bird-friend-number-one flies by and takes it away.

"It's okay to cry, my child," the woman says.

I sniff and shake my head. "Why did this happen to me?"

The woman pats my shoulder but doesn't say anything.

I sniff and swallow snot. "Is it because I was bad?" I look over at her and ask. "Is it because I was mean to Leonard George on the bus?" I feel a drip trying to come out of my nose again, and I suck it up. "I couldn't help myself, you know. It's not my fault he stinks so bad."

The woman looks at me pitifully. She has the most peaceful face I have ever seen in my life, like she's never had a care in the world. And that makeup is so perfect, even Danielle would be proud.

"No," she answers. "We've all been rude a time or two. It's not the worst sin in the book."

I have another question to ask her, but I'm afraid of the answer. So I lower my head and stare at my hands instead. But she obviously already knows what I want to ask, because she takes my hand and says, "No, child. It's not because of your mother either."

I raise my head. "It's not?"

"No," she answers softly. "You didn't transition because you were rude to your mother. Transitioning has nothing to do with being good or bad. Well, in most cases," she adds with a frown.

"Transition?"

She smiles. "It sounds so much lovelier than died, doesn't it?"

I smile, and the woman wipes away the last of my tears with the back of her satin hand. "Plants die, my dear. People transition," she says.

I smile back at her and perk up a bit. As I look around, I can't believe how stunning this place is. It's filled with flowers and blooming trees. I don't know much about flowers, but Mama does. If she were here, she could tell me the name of every one of them. She once had dreams of going to college. To study botany. But that never happened, because of me.

I shake off the thought before I get all sad again.

I want to see more of this place, but this woman doesn't seem to be in any hurry to show me around. She's just sitting here smiling at me with her hands delicately crossed in her lap.

"So, this is Heaven, huh?" I say.

The woman laughs gently and says, "No. You're in Paradise, my child."

"Paradise?"

She smiles and nods.

"Paradise," I say, snapping my fingers. "I've heard of this place before. Something about paradise and Abraham's chest, or bosom, or something like that. Yeah. That's it. I remember because I asked, 'How in the world can a man have a bosom?' And the Sunday school lady kicked me out of class."

The woman throws back her head and laughs.

"You sure I'm supposed to be here?" I ask. "I mean, I haven't been all that good, you know. Just this morning I lied to Mama. Well, technically, I lie to her every morning, because I'm not supposed to wear makeup. But I sneak and put on some of Danielle's every morning anyway."

"Of course you're supposed to be here," she answers. "I received the dispatch just as I sat down to relax with a cup of tea."

She strokes my cheek gently, smiling, studying me so hard that I believe she can see straight through me. I stare back at her. I feel like I've seen her before.

"Wait a minute," I say. "Did you say tea?"

She nods.

"They got tea here?"

The woman winks. "Milk and honey, too."

I lean back onto the bench and smile. "I think I might like it here," I say. "They got Coke?"

"Cherry only," she says.

I frown. "Never mind."

The woman squeezes my hand playfully. "I'm just pulling your leg, darlin'," she says. "We might be able to sneak you a cola now and then. But we'd have to get it from the Earth-realm. We don't have strong drinks here. Except coffee, tea, and hot chocolate, of course. The comfort drinks."

I look at her sideways. "Coffee, tea, and hot chocolate? You pulling my leg again?"

The woman laughs, showing off her perfect white teeth. "No, Jimmy Lee, darlin', I'm not pulling your leg. Coffee, tea, and chocolate have been around since ancient times, so we'll have them forever."

Coffee, tea, and hot chocolate in Heaven, but no Coke? I shake my head. *I don't even wanna think about where they get the milk.*

So, I change the subject. "Why are we here instead of Heaven anyway?"

"Because this is where you transition," the woman answers, making quotation signs with her fingers as she says the word transition. "I'm your guide.

I'll escort you through the gates then show you around."

My heart feels like it skips a beat. "The gates? You mean the *pearly* gates?"

She nods and smiles brightly.

"I really made it to Heaven?"

"Of course you did," she says. "Why wouldn't you?"

"You sure I'm not going to that other place?"

"Oh, Jimmy Lee," she says, chuckling. "What are you so afraid of?"

I shrug. "I don't know. Maybe because Aunt Millie said I was going somewhere else when I died. I mean, *transitioned*. It seemed like every other day, she was wagging her finger in my face saying, 'You better get it right with Jesus, gal, before it's everlastingly and eternally too late.'"

The woman's smile turns into a scowl. "Millicent will be surprised to see a lot of us here, won't she?"

I jump. "Millicent?"

The woman suddenly grabs my hand as if she's been startled, too.

"I'm so sorry, my dear," she says. "I've forgotten my manners. I failed to introduce myself. I know your name, but you don't know mine.

"Jimmy Lee Easton," she says, squeezing my hand gently, "I am Evangeline Shells. Your official guide through the pearly gates and beyond. And I am very pleased to finally make your acquaintance."

I can't help but laugh. "Is that 'shells' like sea shells?" I ask.

"It's exactly like sea shells," the woman answers. "But you, my darlin', may call me *Aunt* Evangeline."

"*Aunt* Evangeline?" I choke. "You're my aunt?"

"Well, technically, I'm your great-aunt," she says. "I'm Millicent's sister."

"Aunt Millie? *My* Aunt Millie?"

Aunt Evangeline nods.

"You're her sister?"

"In the flesh," she answers. "Well, not exactly in the flesh," she corrects. "I'm in my Earth-form."

"You pulling my leg again?"

Aunt Evangeline shakes her head from side to side. She's beaming brighter than a 1,000-watt light bulb.

"Aunt Evangeline," I whisper, too stunned to say anything else.

Now I have a million questions. Earth-form? Paradise? My official guide through the gates? Aunt

Millie's sister? And why is she so fancy and pretty, and Aunt Millie's so plain and ugly?

But all I can do is sit here and stare at her with my mouth hanging open. No wonder she looks so familiar. She looks a little bit like Mama, but nothing like that ugly old Aunt Millie.

I fix my eyes on her. She's so beautiful that I can't stop staring. She seems old, but she doesn't look old. Not like Aunt Millie anyway. I figure she must have died young. So I ask her, "How'd you die? I mean *transition*."

Aunt Evangeline places her hand over her heart and says, "Old age, darlin'."

"But you look so young," I say.

Aunt Evangeline laughs. "Why thank you. That's very kind of you."

She takes my hand in hers and looks dreamily toward the sky. "I was an old lady, all done with my living, when I slipped away in my sleep," she says. "It was a warm, clear night. July 31 to be exact."

I startle. "That's right before my birthday."

"Indeed it is. The same year, too," says Aunt Evangeline. "You know what they say — when a new life is coming, an old one's about to leave."

My face scrunches up. "I made you die?"

-58-

Aunt Evangeline pats my hand. "Heavens no, darlin'. It was just my time to leave, and it was your time to come. I didn't mind giving up my space for someone as lovely as you. Besides, I was already in my seventy-first year." She rests her head on the back of the bench and laughs gently. "It was I who was always saying, 'Three score and ten. If you go past that, you're doing it again.'"

My forehead wrinkles. "I have no idea what that means."

Aunt Evangeline smiles. "Three score and ten, my dear, is seventy years. That's all we're promised. My mother used to say that if we live past that, we're using up somebody else's time."

Goosebumps cover my arms. I'm only twelve. That means I had a lot more time left. I take a minute to do the math in my head. (A long while. Math was not by best subject.) "So," I say, still calculating to make sure I get it right, "that means somebody, or a few somebodies, used up fifty-eight of my years."

Aunt Evangeline laughs. "Well, it certainly wasn't me."

I roll my eyes. "Aunt Millie's as old as black pepper. I can blame her for most of them."

Aunt Evangeline laughs again then closes her eyes like she's reminiscing. I can't believe how beautiful she is. I bet Mama would look like that, too, if she wasn't all stressed out and burning herself up with cigarettes.

Aunt Evangeline smiles and opens her eyes. "It was a lovely night," she says. "After I finished watching my favorite movie, *Mrs. Doubtfire*, I took a warm bubble-bath, sipped a cup of raspberry tea, and retired for the night. I pulled those covers up to my chin and fell into a deep, cozy sleep. When I woke up, I was here—in Paradise," she says, looking around smiling even bigger. "And I was forty-two again."

My eyebrows shoot up. "Forty-two?"

She sees the look on my face and adds, "I know. Forty-two seems old to you young folks. But, honey, when you're seventy, forty-two is primetime. And trust me, darlin'. After that, it's all downhill. If you know what I mean," she says with a wink.

"Seventy, huh?" I say, raising my eyebrows. "And Aunt Millie's already seventy-nine."

"And as strong as a horse," Aunt Evangeline frowns and says. "She'll live to be a hundred."

I groan. "Poor Mama."

Aunt Evangeline smooths down the front of her dress. Surprisingly, a cloud of sadness suddenly covers her face. "My sister never mentioned me, did she?" she asks quietly.

I don't know if it's permitted in Paradise, but I try to stretch the truth anyway. "Well, she—"

Aunt Evangeline pats my hand. "It's okay, darlin'. I know she didn't."

I drop my eyes and quietly tell the truth. "She never told me she had a sister named Evangeline," I say. "She doesn't even mention my grandma. Mama doesn't talk about her either. Aunt Millie acts like she doesn't have any family. Like she just appeared from nowhere."

Aunt Evangeline laughs stiffly. "That's Millicent," she says. "She and I stopped talking a long time ago."

I want to say I'm sorry, because it seems right. But I don't know what I'm sorry for. I would think she'd be grateful that she and Aunt Millie stopped talking. I know I would be.

"Well, Millicent, I should say, stopped talking to me a long time ago," Aunt Evangeline says. "It was always her way or the highway, as they say. So I chose the highway."

"She did that to Mama too," I say. "She stopped talking to her for six months after I was born. All because she didn't like my name."

Aunt Evangeline smiles and touches my cheek with the back of her hand. "I know," she says. "I saw."

"You did?"

Aunt Evangeline nods. "I was right there when it happened. Right there at the hospital the day you were born."

"You were?"

Aunt Evangeline nods.

"Aunt Millie never mentions you when she tells me the story, which is like, every other day."

"That's because she didn't see me," Aunt Evangeline says with a chuckle.

She leans back and rests her head on the bench and smiles. Her lips curl up perfectly, like she's posing for the camera. Aunt Millie probably hated her because she was so beautiful. And, from the looks of that dress, I bet she was rich too.

"Mama says Aunt Millie's so religious that she acts like she's going to Heaven twice or something."

Aunt Evangeline laughs. "My sister, Millicent. Super Saint Extraordinaire. Your grandmother used to tell her the same thing."

"Is my grandmother here?" I ask.

Aunt Evangeline suddenly stops laughing. She sits up straighter than an arrow and crosses her hands in her lap again.

I stare at her, waiting for an answer.

"Well, is she?" I ask again. I frown and say, "Aunt Millie says she's not."

But Aunt Evangeline still doesn't answer me. She just sits there, staring straight ahead like her life depends on it.

I ask her again.

She takes my hand. "I'm sorry, Jimmy Lee," she says quietly. "I'm not allowed to give you that information right now."

Well! I guess I'm not the only one here doing a little truth-stretching.

Misery Loves Company

"The miserable have no other medicine."
~ **Measure for Measure**

Aunt Evangeline sees the look on my face and says, "Well, no time for tears and sad memories. This is a happy place, and we're going to be happy, Jimmy Lee!"

Even though she didn't answer my question, my heart warms again just the same. Aunt Evangeline's smile is so radiant that I can't help but feel good and smile too. I think about Mama and Danielle. I know I'm gonna miss them, but I don't feel sad. For some reason, I just know they'll both be okay without me.

"So if you were seventy the year I was born. That makes you..." I start to calculate on my fingers.

"Three years older than Millicent," Aunt Evangeline answers for me. "And she still tried to tell me how to live my life. The miserable have no other medicine."

I raise my eyebrows. "The miserable have no other medicine?"

Aunt Evangeline pats my hand. "Shakespeare, darlin'. *Measure for Measure*. I don't know what Mr. Shakespeare meant by it. But I know what it means for me: miserable people want to make other people miserable, too."

I nod. "Misery loves company. That's what Mama always says."

"And we both know how miserable Millicent can be," Aunt Evangeline laughs and says.

I shake my head, knowing just how she feels. Aunt Millie goes to church every time the doors are open, and she makes me and Mama go, too. One time I tried to pretend I had a stomachache, and that wicked woman literally dragged me out the door and threw me in the backseat of Lil' Shirl. (That's how we got to church. Ms. Shirley would drop us off and pick us back up.)

And let me tell you. Aunt Millie's church, The Church of the Most Holiest, is the most boring place IN…THE…WORLD. And we still had to go there four times a week. Sunday morning. Monday night.

Wednesday night. And Saturday morning. At 6 a.m. For prayer. Now who wants to pray at 6 o'clock on Saturday morning? Even God took Saturday off and slept in. (I got that one from Mama.)

Just thinking about Aunt Millie rolling in her holiness makes me shudder. So I know I need to change the subject.

"Is that how it is here?" I ask Aunt Evangeline, getting back to her age. "You go back to the best age of your life?"

"Perhaps," Aunt Evangeline answers. "Earthly speaking, that is."

She looks over at me lovingly, her eyes studying my face. She smiles at me, just like Mama used to sometimes when she was in one of her good-mama moods. Then she gently brushes my cheek with the back of her wonderfully soft hand. "But in Heaven," she says, "we don't really have an age."

She takes my hand and places it on my cheek and says, "Feel your face."

I feel my face. I can't believe it! My puffy cheeks are gone! And my skin feels like velvet, just like Aunt Evangeline's hands!

I feel my whole face. All of my features have changed—except my lips. They're still thick.

Aunt Evangeline takes a small round mirror from her purse and hands it to me.

"They got mirrors here, too?"

Aunt Evangeline chuckles. "By special request only, my dear."

I study my face in the mirror. "Wow," I whisper. "I look—"

"About fifteen?" Aunt Evangeline raises her eyebrows and says. "Old enough to wear makeup, perhaps?"

We both laugh like we've just shared the best secret in the world. I guess she was "there" when Mama told me I had to wait till I was fifteen to wear makeup. I reach over and hug her.

I hold the mirror up to my face again. "It's weird," I say, stroking my face, "but I always thought dead people were just *ghosts*. Like you could see straight through them or something."

Aunt Evangeline smiles that warm smile again. She sure doesn't look like a ghost.

"How could I be twelve when I died, then wake-up and be fifteen? It's like I just got transported to another planet and got a new body."

Aunt Evangeline nods. "It's sort of like that. But, you're not really fifteen, my dear. You just look that way. It's *your* perfect form. Your Earth-form. The age you considered perfect. But there's no age here. It's just how we appear after our transitions."

"But how? I never lived to be fifteen."

"But it's the age you longed for," Aunt Evangeline says with a contented sigh.

I study myself in the mirror again. I like what I see. Perfectly arched eyebrows. Long lashes. High cheekbones. I even like my lips, finally. Probably because my cheeks aren't so round. They kind of make me look like one of those models with pouty lips.

Aunt Evangeline nudges me with her elbow. "Hey, be grateful you didn't come here with pimples."

"Yeah, I know," I say with a laugh.

"There was absolutely *nothing* wrong with the way you looked before," says Aunt Evangeline. "You were just as beautiful then as you are now. You just couldn't see that because you were too focused on how everybody else looked."

"I know," I say again. Still, I admire my reflection some more. "My skin is as smooth as silk," I say quietly. "And it's the same color as Mr. Davis's coffee when he pours all that cream in it."

Aunt Evangeline jumps. "Good heavens, I'm glad you mentioned your teacher," she says. "We've been so busy chatting that I forgot about your friend. We've been waiting for you to wake up so we can all go through the gates together."

I give her a puzzled look. "My friend? Danielle? Danielle's here?" I ask anxiously.

"No, no," Aunt Evangeline shakes her head and says. "Not her, darlin'. Your other friend."

What! Not A. J.! *Please, don't let it be A. J.* The thought of seeing that ugly face forever frightens me.

Aunt Evangeline leaps up. "Come along, darlin'. They're waiting for us by the waterfall. We'll enter the gates through there."

"They?" I stand up and ask. "How many of us died—I mean, transitioned?"

Aunt Evangeline's face clouds. "Just you and your friend. And the bus driver. But the bus driver..." She hesitates.

"Mr. Gibbons," I say.

Aunt Evangeline nods then places her hand on my shoulder. "He's not here, Jimmy Lee," she says, regretfully. "He went somewhere else."

A lump fills my throat. "Oh," is all I can say.

But Aunt Evangeline is all smiles again. "This is a happy place," she says. "So let's put sad memories and regrets behind us and get to that waterfall."

I smile and agree. Maybe A. J. will be nicer here than she was on Earth. But I still think she should've gone on with Mr. Gibbons, seeing how evil she was.

Mar What's Well?

"Striving to better, oft we mar what's well."
~ **King Lear**

This place, Paradise, is so beautiful that I can hardly breathe. Now I finally know what Mr. Davis meant when he'd describe something as breath-taking. This place really is taking my breath away.

Flowers are everywhere. And they're so pretty and smell so good. They're pink and purple and red and yellow and blue. And some colors I don't even know. And the trees. Wow. Greener than anything I've ever seen.

And the birds here—they aren't just chirping. I can tell they're actually singing.

"Lovely, isn't it?" Aunt Evangeline asks.

"Yes," I say, looking around like a little kid in a toy store.

As we head to the waterfall, I see other sitting areas like the one I was in. And there are people there, too. Some are on benches. Some are in gazebos. And some are just standing under trees. They're all hugging and chatting like Aunt Evangeline and I were doing— having their happy little family reunions.

We pass an old couple in a gazebo. Aunt Evangeline gasps. "There's Randolph Martin," she says. "We came here at the same time."

Aunt Evangeline smiles and waves. The old man waves back. "Randolph's been waiting a long time for his wife Marie to join him," she says. "I'm glad she finally came."

"How come they came here old?" I ask. "Why would anybody want an old body in Heaven?"

"Because that's when they were happiest," replies Aunt Evangeline. She stops for a moment and looks at the old man and his wife. She has her hand to her chest, and she looks like she might cry. But she's smiling.

"That's not the body Marie died in," she says. "That's the body she had when Randolph left her on Earth. That's the body he remembers. That poor old body Marie left on Earth was nothing more than a raggedy bag of bones."

Aunt Evangeline sighs then moves on. "I'm glad she finally left it."

I can hear the sound of the waterfall getting closer, but I'm not really ready to leave this place. It's so peaceful. "Do people sometimes just stay here?" I ask Aunt Evangeline.

"Oh, honey, why would anyone want to stay here when they got Heaven?" Aunt Evangeline replies. "It's much grander."

My heart leaps. "Are the streets really made of gold?"

She takes my hand. "Why don't you come find out for yourself?"

And there's the waterfall. Now I really can't breathe. The waterfall is flowing out of the side of a mountain—a mountain covered with thick grass, like a plush green carpet. There are flowers here, too. And trees. The colors are so vivid and beautiful. So amazing.

The way the water flows through the flowers and trees on the mountain and splashes on the rocks below makes it all seem unreal, like a dream. The water looks so clean and refreshing that I want to run to it.

But I don't. I walk at the same pace as Aunt Evangeline, who is taking her own sweet time. I guess when you got forever, there's no need to be in a hurry.

"I wish I could take a picture and send it to Mama," I say. "She would love this." Then I start to feel sad again, because I had been so mean to Mama right before the field trip. I know she was only trying to show that she loved me, but most times she simply tried my nerves. I never got to go anywhere unless she was with me. No movies. No school parties. No field trips. Nothing. Now I feel guilty that I wanted to get away from her so badly.

Aunt Evangeline stops. She turns to me. "I know what you're thinking."

"You can read my mind?"

"Not exactly," says Aunt Evangeline. "But you give off such strong vibes that I can sense your thoughts." She hesitates then says, "I know how you feel about Darlynn. And you shouldn't."

I'm not sure if she means she knows that I feel guilty or she knows that Mama got on my nerve. So I ask her.

"Both," she answers. She then turns and continues on to the waterfall.

After a few seconds, she says, "Striving to better, oft we mar what's well."

"Shakespeare?"

"But, of course," Aunt Evangeline answers. "*King Lear.*"

"And it means?"

Aunt Evangeline stops. Placing her hands on my shoulders, she turns me to face her. Her expression is totally serious. "It means you can ruin something that's already good by constantly trying to make it better."

She stares at me for a moment, giving me time to get what she just said. Then she frowns and says, "Your mother has been around Millicent too long."

She drops her hands from my shoulders then starts walking again.

I follow her. "I never want to forget this waterfall," I say, trying to make myself forget about Mama.

Aunt Evangeline chuckles. "You won't forget it, darlin'. Besides, I'm sure you'll be sent here to meet someone, just like I was sent to meet you."

"I'll probably meet Mama," I say. And the thought makes me feel a little better.

Aunt Evangeline points to two figures standing right under the waterfall. "There they are," she says.

I can barely see them because of the water, but I see two people running playfully through the water. I shake my head. "That's not A. J. That's a boy."

"Who's A. J.?" Aunt Evangeline asks.

"My friend," I answer. "Well, Danielle's friend, actually. But we all hang out together on account of Danielle. But I really can't stand A. J. So when you said my friend was here and it wasn't Danielle, I figured you meant A. J."

"Well, since you two came together and the fellow waited all this time to go through the gates with you, I assumed you were friends," Aunt Evangeline says.

I look at her suspiciously. "You don't mean boyfriend, do you?"

Aunt Evangeline laughs. "No, darlin'. I mean *friend* friend. He woke up as soon as he was transitioned. Actually, I'm not sure he ever fell asleep. I think he soared here with his eyes wide open," she says. "But, you, my darlin'. Oh, you nearly slept through a whole day. And that boy still wanted to wait for you."

"I slept a whole day?"

"Indeed you did," answers Aunt Evangeline.

"I thought there was no night time in Heaven."

"Well, we're not in Heaven yet, dear. But there's no night here either," Aunt Evangeline says. "But the sun still rises and sets. It just never gets dark."

"Look at that," she says, pointing west of the waterfall.

The waterfall has been so captivating that I hadn't noticed the sunset. The sun is sitting like a huge orange ball, glowing on the horizon. "It's beautiful," I whisper.

"Do you like sunsets, Jimmy Lee?" Aunt Evangeline asks quietly.

"Yes," I answer, never taking my eyes off that wonderful sunset.

"Me too," Aunt Evangeline says.

"When I was little, Mama and I used to sit outside in the grass some evenings and watch the sun set. The sun would always disappear so quickly. I hated to see the day end."

"You don't have to worry about that here. The sunsets are very long. The sun never disappears. It just sits there on the horizon until the beginning of a new day. Then it rises on the other side of Paradise."

"Really?"

"Really."

"Is the sunrise long, too?"

"Oh, yes. And truly magnificent."

"Can I come back to Paradise sometime? I want to see the sun rise."

"Of course, you can. But once you see the light of Heaven, you won't really care to come back."

"Really?"

Aunt Evangeline turns me to face her. "Honey, Heaven is so spectacular that it'll make this place look like a dump."

I can't help but laugh as Aunt Evangeline takes my hand and we head toward the waterfall.

The two figures playing in the water see us and wave. So we wave back. The shorter one—my friend, I assume—leaves the water and runs toward us. It's weird, but he's wearing a bright orange T-shirt and navy shorts. Nobody on the bus was wearing shorts. Mr. Davis specifically told everyone to wear jeans. And I know I would've remembered that fluorescent T-shirt. The other weird thing is that his clothes look dry.

"Jimmy Lee!" he calls, waving. And I immediately recognize the voice. It's Poop Boy. And, except for the T-shirt and shorts, it doesn't look like he's changed one bit.

Earth on Heaven

"There are more things in heaven and earth,
Horatio, than are dreamt of in your philosophy."
~ Hamlet

Poop Boy walks toward me with his arms outstretched like he's ready for a hug or something. "Isn't this the most beautiful waterfall you've ever seen?" he asks.

I roll my eyes. "It's the only waterfall I've ever seen."

I don't mean to be so ugly. But how can I not be? I'm stuck in eternity with the most annoying boy from school. And he smells like poop. Why couldn't it have been Carlos Trujillo? He's annoying too, but at least he smells like cologne.

Oh, the nerve! Poop Boy walks up and puts his arms around me. Eeeeew! I just want to get to Heaven, and he's ruining everything, just like the field trip.

Well, I guess that wasn't really his fault. I should blame Mr. Gibbons for that.

I instinctively pull back without thinking. Then I'm ashamed of myself when I see the look on Aunt Evangeline's face. She almost looks like Aunt Millie for a second.

"Hi, Leonard," I say awkwardly, trying to redeem myself.

Poop Boy flashes me a broad smile. And somehow those once corn-yellow teeth are now whiter than Aunt Millie's big, old-lady bloomers that she hangs over the shower rod every night.

"Your teeth—" I say, before I catch myself. Now I'm seriously wanting to take a sniff to see if he smells better, too. I know he looks better—not cute like Carlos—but neat, like he's finally taken a good bath and scrubbed off all that grime. I wonder how long he was under that waterfall.

The other person from the waterfall comes up behind Poop Boy. He looks like an older version of him. He also looks like a black Mr. Rogers from *Mr. Rogers Neighborhood*. So I assume he's Poop Boy's grandpa. But Poop Boy turns around and says, "This is my pop, Jimmy Lee."

My mouth flies open, but I catch myself and hurry up and close it. The man extends his hand toward me like he wants me to shake it. But when I get closer, he grabs me in a bear hug like Poop Boy did.

Eeeeew! Two poop hugs in less than a minute.

But wait. Did I catch the scent of spice? I sniff, trying not to be too obvious. Poop Boy's daddy smells like Mr. Davis. *Sniff. Sniff.* Like apples and cinnamon.

I turn around and hug Poop Boy again. "I'm happy you're here with me," I lie. *Sniff.* Not a hint of poop. Heaven *is* a wonderful place.

But he'll always be Poop Boy to me, no matter how good he smells.

"Are we all ready to go?" Papa Poop asks.

"Wait," I say, stepping away from Poop Boy. I look at him. Then I look at his daddy. "Your daddy's *dead?*"

"Not anymore," Poop Boy answers, grinning sarcastically. And Aunt Evangeline thinks it's funny.

"You know what I mean," I say. "You didn't tell me your daddy was dead. I thought you said he took you to the Civil Rights Museum."

Papa Poop puts his arm around Poop Boy's shoulders. "I did take him to the Civil Rights Museum," he says, smiling, admiring his son like he's made of gold. "But that was a long time ago. When I still had my health."

"And your breath," Poop Boy says. Then he cracks up worse than A.J.

Papa Poop laughs with him.

I hope their mansion is far, far away from mine.

"So you lived with your mama?" I ask Poop Boy, breaking up the party.

"No. I lived with my wicked stepmother and my two wicked stepbrothers," he says.

I wait for him to laugh, but he doesn't. His daddy doesn't either.

"I'm glad I'm here with my pop now," he says, hugging his daddy and returning the admiration.

I glance at Aunt Evangeline, and she smiles knowingly. Then I feel bad about calling him Poop Boy.

Oh well, old habits are hard to break.

"Hey, did you see my gazebo!" Poop Boy beams.

"I saw a bunch of gazebos," I say dryly.

"Mine is a big white one with my name on it."

"Really?"

Aunt Evangeline chuckles. "He's just pulling your leg, darlin'," she says. "His name is on a bunch of the gazebos. The benches, too." She motions toward Papa Poop. "Mr. George is one of our carpenters. He takes pride in his work, and he likes to put his name on it."

"So they all say 'Leonard'?" I ask.

Papa Poop shakes his head. "Not all of them. Just the ones I build."

"Wow," I say. "I didn't know people actually got to do stuff in Heaven."

Papa Poop laughs. "Don't believe all that hype about angels floating around on clouds, Miss Jimmy Lee. Life really does go on. Everything we did on Earth prepared us for our new life in Heaven. Well, almost everything," he adds.

"There are more things in Heaven and Earth, Horatio, than are dreamt of in your philosophy," Aunt Evangeline says.

"*Hamlet!*" Papa Poop beams.

I cross my arms and glare at him. "You into this Shakespeare fellow, too?"

"Who isn't?" Poop Boy chimes in.

I feel an eye-roll coming on. "Heaven, help us," I mutter.

"Speaking of Heaven," Poop Boy says, "shouldn't we be going through the gates?" He checks his wrist. I guess old habits really are hard to break.

I'm anxious to see what my mansion looks like too. Well, I assume I have a mansion, since that's what Aunt Millie always talked about—her mansion in the sky. She'd always walk through the apartment singing, *"I've got a mansion just over the hilltop in that bright land where we'll never grow old,"* which, by the way, was too late for her.

I never understood why she wouldn't move out of that apartment if a mansion was what she really wanted to live in. Well, I always wanted to live in a mansion too, and now I was finally going to. But I sure do wish Mama could be with me. I know that's pretty selfish, seeing she'd have to die to get here. But I just know she'd like it. Then she wouldn't have to be so stressed and worried all the time. And she wouldn't have to look at Aunt Millie's sour old face anymore either.

Boy, I wish she could see this sunset and the waterfall. The way that big orange ball is sitting low on a peaceful horizon and the way the cool water is splashing down the side of the plush, green mountainside almost makes me want to stay right here in Paradise.

But leave it to Poop Boy to spoil the moment. He grabs my hand and says, "You think this is something. Wait till you see the gates."

Then he drags me right into the waterfall.

To Be or Not to Be

"To be, or not to be, — that is the question."
~ Hamlet

This place is so AWE-*SOME*! We're inside a waterfall, but there's no water falling! Just peace and brightness and beauty and singing angels. Real angels! Real live glowing angels! With wings and harps and trumpets and ... *saxophones*?

And they're not singing the old-timey music Aunt Millie is always listening to either. It's cool music. Well, not cool like a rock-star or rapper kind of cool. But cool in a God kind of way. A jazzy-holy cool.

I feel like jumping up and down, and Aunt Evangeline notices the glow in me. "It's delightful, isn't it, darlin'?"

All I can do is beam and nod.

It's like we've stepped into a whole other dimension. Well, I guess we have! Outside the waterfall is the vibrant garden. And inside, right here as we step inside, is the lush green mountainside, with birds chirping and angels singing, and people walking through the most magnificent gates that probably anyone on Earth has ever seen.

The gates are taller than Clark-Cooke Middle, which is two stories high! And maybe just as wide! And the color is the same as Mrs. Aberdeen's Cadillac. Polished pearl white is what she calls it. There's no sun, but the light is brilliant. And its reflection off the pearly gates is causing a rainbow of colors to flow down over us.

One of the angels begins to play "When the Saints Go Marching In" on the saxophone, and I begin to cry. Aunt Millie has sung that song a thousand times, and it's never sounded this good. I know Aunt Evangeline said there were no tears in this place, but I can't help it. I've never felt so free and happy before.

Leonard puts his arm around my shoulders and leads me toward the gates. He suddenly seems like the kindest person ever, and I know I'll never call him Poop Boy again. *Maybe.*

Aunt Evangeline and Mr. George follow us. And right behind us is the couple we saw in the garden, the old people who are friends with Aunt Evangeline. I hear the old man humming "When the Saints Go Marching In", and his wife is singing the words. Her voice doesn't even sound old.

Right at the entrance of the gates is a whole family—a man and a woman and two little kids, a boy and a girl. They look Asian. But as soon as they go through the gates, they change. And I can't tell what they are! They don't look Black, White, Asian, Mexican, or anything else. They're just *people*. Their skin is almost translucent. And they're *glowing*.

I stop dead in my tracks. "Did you see that?" I ask no one in particular.

Aunt Evangeline chuckles. "They're in Heaven-form, dear," she replies. "What you saw before was Earth-form."

Leonard steps away from me and says, "You and Pop keep saying that. What exactly does that mean?"

Aunt Evangeline and Mr. George step to the side and allow the old couple, Mr. Martin and his wife, Marie, to pass.

"Earth-form is how we appear to people on Earth," Aunt Evangeline answers. "Otherwise, they wouldn't recognize us."

"And we'd scare the living daylights out of 'em," Mr. George says.

"And Heaven-form is just what it sounds like," says Aunt Evangeline. "It's how we appear in Heaven."

"Flesh and blood cannot inherit the kingdom of God," Mr. George says. "We only look like people on Earth. But we've actually been changed into something totally different."

I side-eye Leonard. "No kidding," I say under my breath.

"Well, I've waited long enough," he says. He bolts toward the gates. "I wanna see what I really look like in there."

His daddy grabs him by the collar. "Hold on, partner." He waves me forward. "Ladies first."

Aunt Evangeline comes up beside me and takes my hand. "Let's go in together."

Right after Mr. and Mrs. Martin enter in, we step forward. But just as we step across the threshold, Aunt Evangeline's form changes instantly and I fall backward like I just walked into a brick wall.

"Jimmy Lee!" Leonard cries.

He reaches down and helps me up.

Aunt Evangeline turns and comes back through the gate, changing instantly back into Earth-form. "What happened, darlin'?"

"I don't know." I rub my head. I can't believe it actually hurts. "It was like I just walked into a wall or something."

Leonard waves his hand across the threshold to show me there's no wall, just empty space. I press my own hand forward, and it feels like I hit a windowpane. Aunt Evangeline and Mr. George do the same thing, and their hands wave in the air. No wall. No windowpane.

I try again. Same thing.

"What's happening?" I ask Aunt Evangeline.

My lips quiver, and I know I'm about to cry again. Only this time, they're not tears of joy. "Why won't my hand go through?"

Aunt Evangeline crosses the threshold again, goes straight through, and instantly changes. She comes back out. "Try again, dear."

I try again and fall flat on my bottom when I hit the invisible wall. "I can't go through," I mutter. I bury my face in my hands and sob.

Leonard sits down on the ground beside me and puts his arm around my shoulders. He doesn't say anything. He just sits with me while I cry.

"Why can't I get in?"

"Because you're not dead yet," comes a voice from the other side of the gates.

Leonard jumps to his feet. "What? Who said that?"

"I did," the voice comes again. And out steps a surfer-dude sporting gold hair, a dark tan, a Hawaiian shirt, and khaki shorts. Oh yeah, and flip flops.

"What do you mean she's not dead yet?" Mr. George asks.

Mr. Hawaii rolls his eyes. "She's. Not. Dead. Yet," he says.

I jump to my feet, and my tears dry up as quickly as they came. "I'm not?" I choke.

"No, honey, you're not," Mr. Hawaii answers, waving his hand. "You're half-dead."

"She is not *half-dead*," Leonard retorts. "She's dead. And I died trying to save her."

"You did?" I ask.

Mr. Hawaii holds his hand up to Leonard. "High-five, dude. That was quite a heroic feat you accomplished down there, trying to save your girlfriend and all. But she's still not dead."

"I'm not his girlfriend," I say. But nobody's paying me any attention.

"How can she be here if she's not dead?" asks Aunt Evangeline.

Mr. Hawaii shrugs. "Lots of folks get to this point. It's called *'near-death experience',*" he adds sarcastically. "You know—the light at the end of the tunnel, seeing the dead relatives, floating through the air on clouds—all that jazz."

"No, no, no," I say, shaking my head. "I'm dead. I hit my head. I fell asleep. I slept a whole day. I had weird dreams. I woke up. I'm fifteen. I'm pretty. And I'm dead."

"No, no, no," Mr. Hawaii shakes his finger at me and says. "You hit your head. You injured your brain. It stopped working. Blood stopped flowing to the rest of your body. You died for a moment, and your spirit slipped away. A paramedic resuscitated you, but your spirit didn't go back. They hooked you up to a machine. It's keeping your heart pumping. And the folks in charge here sent me to take you back."

Aunt Evangeline gasps. "Take her back?"

I cross my arms with a huff. "What if I don't wanna go back?"

Mr. Hawaii laughs. "They figured you'd say that." He shakes his head. "Nobody ever wants to go back, honey."

Mr. George snorts. "Can you blame 'em?"

Leonard chimes in. "What about me? Am I dead?"

"Oh, goodness, yes," Mr. Hawaii answers. "You died instantly, as soon as you hit that tree. There was no resuscitating that body."

"Gee, thanks," Leonard says under his breath.

"How'd you hit a tree?" I ask.

Leonard barely has his mouth open before Mr. Hawaii answers for him. "When he saw you flying toward the front of the bus, he jumped up and tried to save you. But the impact that slammed you into the dashboard sent him flying out the window. Straight into a tree. It was the most heroic thing I'd ever seen. Better than Romeo and Juliet."

"I'm not his girl—"

"But, sadly, you can't stay," Mr. Hawaii interrupts.

"But I don't wanna go back," I say again.

"Does she have to?" Leonard asks.

I hope he's not taking this girlfriend thing seriously.

"Well, that was the plan originally. But since her mother's down there having a fit, we've decided to send her back."

"Who's *we?*" Aunt Evangeline asks defiantly.

Mr. Hawaii gives her a look that says, "*Are you kidding me?*"

"How can I *not* be dead?" I ask. "I've been here a whole day."

"That's in *Paradise* days, sweetheart," Mr. Hawaii corrects. "You've been half-dead for only an hour on Earth."

"An hour?" Leonard peeps.

"Yep. It's still Friday, May 13. And the time is only 10:20 a.m."

"Wow," Leonard whispers. He checks that imaginary watch again. "Only one hour, huh."

Aunt Evangeline slips her arm around me and pulls me close to her. "It's okay, Jimmy Lee, dear. We'll straighten this out."

"Yes, we sure will," Mr. Hawaii says as he pries me from Aunt Evangeline's embrace. "Now you people just run along to your mansions, and I'll take Little

Miss back to her mama. Shoo, shoo, run along now," he says, waving them off.

"We're not going anywhere without Jimmy Lee," Leonard says.

"That's right," his daddy chimes in.

Mr. Hawaii plants his hands on his hips. "Look, people," he says, rolling his eyes. "There's a woman down there praying her heart out for this child's return, and it is my job to take her back. So I'd appreciate your cooperation in this matter, or I'll be forced to take action."

By this time all the angels have stopped singing and playing their instruments. And they're staring at us like they're ready to kick us out for stirring up trouble—like they did the devil and his posse.

I don't wanna take any chances, so I just take a deep breath and say, "I'll go back."

"No!" Leonard cries. "You can't go back. Why would you want to go back? People are so *mean* down there."

"I have a mama down there who wants me back," I mumble.

"Why can't her mama just come here?" Leonard asks Mr. Hawaii.

Mr. Hawaii rolls his eyes. "What do I look like to you? The Death Angel? I don't take souls *from* Earth. I take displaced souls back *to* Earth. And you people are making my job extremely difficult. Now if *y'all* don't mind, I'd like to take Little Miss back to her mama, because I've got thirteen other displaced souls I've got to get back to their bodies today."

"Oh, Jimmy Lee," Aunt Evangeline says. She grabs me in a hug. "I'm so sorry. I so wanted to show you my theater."

My eyebrows shoot up. "Your *theater*? You have a *theater*?"

"Why, yes, darlin'. Didn't I tell you? I was an actress. The theater was my life."

I shoot a look at Mr. Hawaii, my eyes pleading. But he looks as impatient as Mr. Davis on test day. I try anyway. "Can't I just go in for a little while and see my aunt's theater?"

Mr. Hawaii laughs like I just told the joke of the year. "No can do, Little Miss," he says, wagging his finger at me. "You absolutely cannot cross that threshold."

"Aw, come on, Chuck," Aunt Evangeline begs. "Be a saint. Let her visit for a minute."

"Chuck?" I gasp. I glance at Mr. Hawaii then back at Aunt Evangeline. "You know this guy?"

Chuck waves his hand. "Everybody knows me, honey. I'm a Transport Angel. I find the lost souls and take them to their proper homes."

"Well, Chuck," I say. "May I please go in and visit for a minute."

"Honey, if it were possible, I'd let you do it," he says. "But it's not. Once you cross that threshold, your spirit leaves that old body down there on Earth forever. There's no turning back. Go through those gates, and you hit the big time, baby. Eternity. For. Ever."

Mr. George raises his index finger. "To be, or not to be," he says. "That is the question."

I swallow hard. That's a quote I know. Mr. Davis says it every time one of us raises our hand with a question. It's from Shakespeare's play *Hamlet*. Mr. Davis says that Hamlet dude was trying to decide whether he wanted to live or die. Now I know how he felt.

The look on Aunt Evangeline's face is breaking my heart. So I don't know if I want to go back. Besides, Leonard is right. People are mean. And I have no friends. A. J. is really Danielle's best friend. They have been for years. I was only getting in the way. I don't blame A. J. for hating me.

And Mama and Aunt Millie are so over-protective that I can't ever have fun anyway. Aunt Millie won't even let me go to the movies! If Aunt Evangeline has her own theater, I can watch movies anytime I want. I just hope they're not all a bunch of cheesy, church-themed movies like the ones Aunt Millie watches.

I take a deep breath, then exhale. "I don't want to go back," I say. "I'm staying here."

No More Heartache

"To die, to sleep, —
No more; and by a sleep to say we end
The heart-ache, and the thousand natural shocks
That flesh is heir to, — 'tis a consummation
Devoutly to be wish'd. To die, to sleep."
~ Hamlet

Chuck frowns at me. "Some of you make this job so darned difficult."

Aunt Evangeline takes my hand. "It's okay to go back, Jimmy Lee. Go back and grow up. As you can see, you'll be a beautiful young lady. Then one day, perhaps you'll get married, start a family, enjoy a career. All those wonderful things. And Heaven will be right here waiting for you when you're all done with your living."

Aunt Evangeline makes it all sound so easy, but she has no idea what it's like living with Aunt Millie and Mama, who one minute, sasses Aunt Millie to her face, then the next minute acts like she's scared to death to break one of her rules. And she has no idea what it's like to live in a place called estates, when everybody knows it's just the projects.

Plus I can't ever listen to any cool music or watch anything on TV except religious stuff. And don't get me started on my outdated clothes. Ms. Shirley dresses better than me.

I still got six more years before I can leave that place. Then who's to say I won't turn out like Mama anyway.

"I don't want to go back," I say firmly. "It's my body. I should be able to choose if I want to go back to it or not."

Chuck rolls his eyes and sighs. "You're just special, aren't you?"

"So I can stay?" I ask.

"Well, yes. And no," Chuck answers. "Yes, we could let you stay, because it is your choice. And no, because the folks in charge want to honor your mother's request."

"So you're taking her back?" Leonard asks.

"You people are the most difficult group I've ever run into," Chuck says. He shakes his head. "The problem is that she's stayed too long already. And she should've never been awakened in the first place," he says, glancing narrow-eyed at Aunt Evangeline. "I could've simply taken her back where she belonged, and she would've never known the difference."

"Sorry," Aunt Evangeline mutters.

"But I tell you what I'll do. I'll go in and speak with the folks in charge. They might let you stay, seeing that yours isn't the first displaced soul that hasn't wanted to return to its body."

"Oh, thank you." I gush and reach toward him for a hug.

Chuck quickly jumps back and throws up his hands. "No hugging, Little Miss." He turns up his nose and looks me up and down. "You're still Earth-contaminated."

"But I hugged them," I say, motioning toward Aunt Evangeline and Mr. George.

Chuck rolls his neck and snaps his fingers. "That's their problem," he says, then he turns and goes back through the gate.

"What a hoot!" Mr. George says.

Aunt Evangeline puts her arm around my shoulders. "I'm so sorry, Jimmy Lee. I didn't know I wasn't supposed to wake you. I've brought you here and gotten your hopes up. Now you might have to go back."

"It's okay," I mumble. "If I have to go back, then I'll go back."

The angels have started playing their music again. They're playing "Amazing Grace" and it sounds really good on the saxophone. I so wish I didn't have to go back. I wish Mama could just come here instead.

I saunter over to the side of the mountain and sit on a rock. The rest of the gang follows me. Aunt Evangeline takes my hand in hers. I see she's not afraid of my Earth cooties, unlike Chuck. I rest my head on her shoulder. "Want to hear something funny?" I ask.

"We could use a good joke right now," Mr. George says.

"When I was living, I was scared of dying," I say. "But now that I'm dead, or half-dead, I'm scared to go back to living. I guess I just don't want to have to die twice."

"Who could blame you?" Mr. George says.

Aunt Evangeline leans back on a rock and closes her eyes. "To die, to sleep, no more," she says.

"...and by a sleep to say we end," says Mr. George.

Then Aunt Evangeline says, "The heartache, and the thousand natural shocks that flesh is heir to..."

Mr. George: "…'tis a consummation devoutly to be wish'd."

Aunt Evangeline opens her eyes and sits up straight. Then they both say together, "To die, to sleep—To sleep, perchance to dream:—ay, there's the rub!"

"Let me guess," I say, glaring at them. "*Hamlet.*"

They both smile with contentment.

"Oh well," I say. "I guess it beats listening to Aunt Millie trying to sing."

Thankless Child

*"How sharper than a serpent's tooth it is to have a
thankless child!"*
~ **King Lear**

It seems like it's taking Chuck forever to come back.
But it's only a few minutes, because the angels have
just finished playing "Amazing Grace" and are now
playing "When the Saints Go Marching In" on the
trumpet. Too bad Aunt Millie can't hear it, so she could
know what real music sounds like.

We all jump to our feet and hurry over to Chuck
when he comes through the gates.

"What's the verdict?" Mr. George asks.

"Well, I've got good news and bad news," Chuck
answers. "The good news is that it is your choice
whether you go or stay, since you've been here nearly a

whole day already. The bad news is that you can't make that decision until after you've done two things."

"What?" I ask eagerly.

Chuck crosses his arms and glares at me. He doesn't crack a smile. He stays that way for a few seconds then takes a deep breath. "Please, don't interrupt me when I'm talking."

"Sorry," I mumble.

Chuck smiles. "That's better. Now, first of all, Little Miss, you'll have to go back to the Earth-realm and see what's going on."

Aunt Evangeline nudges me. "You'll like Earth-spying."

Chuck rolls his eyes at her and continues, "Second, there are a couple of people in the Spirit-realm who need to talk to you before you make your decision."

"What people?" Aunt Evangeline interrupts again.

Chuck glares at her. "People who have information she might want to know before she makes her choice." He turns to me. "So, you've got till the next sunset to make up your mind. And, on the sunrise of the third day, you get to choose to go or stay."

"I don't understand why I can't just choose now," I say.

"Because that's not how it works," Chuck answers tersely. "You'll go back to Paradise and wait there. Three people will come see you between now and the next sunset. They'll tell you some things you need to know. And you can take it from there."

"That doesn't make any sense. Why can't you just let me be dead? I don't wanna go back."

I stamp my foot and march back over to my rock and sulk.

One of the angels nods to the other. She nods back, turns to her harp and starts playing some sad song. And it's not even a church song at that.

Chuck marches over and stands in front of me. His face suddenly changes, and he looks just like Aunt Millie!

I gasp and nearly fall off my rock.

"Why you thankless child!" he says in Aunt Millie's voice.

Aunt Evangeline rushes over and gets right in front of Chuck's horrible, Aunt-Millie-like face. "That's not going to help the situation one bit, now is it, Chuck?" she says.

With a scowl, Chuck says to Aunt Evangeline, "How sharper than a serpent's tooth it is to have a thankless child!" Then he snaps his fingers, turns back into himself and says, "*King Lear,* baby. You're not the only one who knows Shakespeare."

Aunt Evangeline snorts.

Chuck narrows his eyes at me and says, "Take it or leave it, Little Miss."

"Okay. Okay. I'll take it."

"Good. We have an understanding." Chuck squints at Aunt Evangeline. "The rest of you can go on to your mansions."

I grab Aunt Evangeline's arm. "But I don't want to stay by myself."

Chuck sighs and rolls his eyes. "You people," he mutters. "Stay," he orders, waving us off. "All of you."

He turns to leave, then stops abruptly and frowns at me. "I'll see you on the third day, Little Miss."

Leonard waves at him. "Aloha!"

"Whatever," Chuck grumbles. He flip-flops off and disappears inside the pearly gates.

No Hooking Up in Heaven

*"I say, we will have no more marriages: those that
are married already, — all but one, — shall live;
the rest shall keep as they are."*
~ **Hamlet**

Okay, Leonard is just "dying" to show me his
gazebo, so we head on back over there. And even
though there are a ton of gazebos around here,
Leonard's does appear to be bigger than everybody
else's. Hmmm. I wonder why. All four of us are sitting
here, and there's still room to spare.

I hadn't really noticed before, but without all
that dirt and grime, Leonard is actually kind of cute.
Not quite as cute as Carlos Trujillo, but still cute. And I
don't know why I'm even thinking about Carlos. He
likes Danielle. Besides that, I'm dead anyway, well,

almost. And who wants a dead girlfriend? Other than Leonard....

Every time I happen to look his way, I catch him staring at me. I sure hope he doesn't seriously think I'm his girlfriend just because Mr. Hawaii said so. I mean, it really would be perfect if I *happened* to like him, seeing how wonderfully romantic the sunset is. But Leonard? The angel formerly known as Poop Boy? No way. Besides, Aunt Millie says there's no such thing as romance in Heaven...which reminds me of a question I had for Aunt Evangeline.

"How come Mr. Martin and his wife went to Heaven together?" I ask. "Aunt Millie says there's no marriage in Heaven. So husbands and wives won't know each other as husbands and wives when they get there."

"Tsk!" Aunt Evangeline says. "What does she know?"

Surprisingly, Aunt Evangeline purses her lips and frowns. "Millicent's just jealous she won't have a husband to reunite with in Heaven."

I'm stunned. I didn't know Aunt Evangeline could get an attitude.

"Of course Randolph knows Marie as his wife, but they don't have the same husband-wife relationship they had on Earth. They're both angels, living independently, without the cares and concerns of marriage," Aunt Evangeline says, her face relaxing some.

"Did you have a husband?" I ask.

Aunt Evangeline closes her eyes and smiles. "Yes, darlin'," she says. "I had three."

"Are they here?" Leonard asks.

Aunt Evangeline smiles again. "One of them is here," she says. "One of them is still on Earth. And the third, unfortunately, chose not to come here."

"How could he *choose* not to come?" Leonard asks.

Aunt Evangeline shrugs. "When he chose not to believe, he chose not to come. It's as simple as that. You can't go somewhere you don't believe exists."

"So when your other husband gets here, which one will you choose?" Leonard asks.

Aunt Evangeline throws back her head and laughs. "You're just like those Sadducees in the Bible days, dear Leonard." She was laughing so hard she could barely get her words out. "'The people of this age marry and are given in marriage. But those who are considered worthy of taking part in the age to come and in the resurrection from the dead will neither marry nor be given in marriage ... for they are like the angels.'"

"That's from the bible, right?" I ask.

Aunt Evangeline nods.

Then Mr. George stands and clears his throat. "I say, we will have no more marriages," he says, his head held high like he's in a Broadway production. "Those that are married already, — all but one, — shall live; the rest shall keep as they are."

"*Hamlet!*" Leonard beams.

Mr. George takes a bow and sits back down.

Aunt Evangeline turns to Leonard and says, "Honey, I'm an angel. My first husband Henry is an angel. My second husband Bob is not. And my third husband John will be one day, I hope. I will still recognize both Henry and John for who they were to me on Earth, and I can still fellowship with them in this wonderful place. But, honey, *thank God*, I don't have to share my mansion with either one of them."

"O-o-o-ka-a-a-y," I say. "Guess that's enough about marriage in Heaven."

"Ditto," Leonard says. "I'm sorry, Ms. Evangeline. I didn't mean to upset you."

Aunt Evangeline waves a red handkerchief at Leonard. "Oh, you didn't upset me, darlin'. I just don't want you to be like those Sadducees. They're so... sad, you see."

"That's a good one, Aunt Evangeline," I say, laughing.

We're all so busy laughing that we don't notice the woman walking toward Leonard's gazebo.

...until she stops and starts smacking her gum like she's trying to work the sweetness out of it.

What's Done Is Done

"What's done is done."
~ **Macbeth**

We all stop laughing. Just like that. No chuckling. No last-second giggling. Nothing. And the only sound left is gum-smacking. Even the birds are quiet.

"Well, if it isn't little Jimmy Lee Easton," the woman says. She pops her gum real loud then walks toward me, completely ignoring everybody else. She sits beside me and grabs my hand. "Lordy!" she breathes. "When they told me you were here, I said, 'Jimmy Lee Easton? That sweet little girl? Why, she can't be any more'n about twelve-years-old.'" Then she sighs and looks me in the eyes and says, "What're you doing here so soon, sweetie?"

I stare at her. I've never seen this woman before in my life. She has flaming, curly red hair piled high on top of her head, with curly ringlets framing her face. She's wearing more makeup than me and Danielle and A.J. put together. And to top it all off, she's wearing one of those old-fashioned nurse's uniforms like you'd see in a movie. With white pantyhose and thick white shoes to match.

I glance at her sideways. "Who are you?"

She places her hand on her chest, her flaming red nails matching her hair. "Why, I'm Brenda Jo Carmichael, sweetie. I'm the nurse who attended your mama when you were born."

I gasp. "You're the—"

"Gum-smacking nurse your aunt's talking about every time she tells the story of how you ended up with a boy's name."

We both laugh, and Nurse Brenda opens her arms to me for a hug. I hug her and notice that she smells like strawberries. Must be all the red.

I have a thought and pull back. "You're dead already?" I ask. "How old were you when I was born?"

Nurse Brenda waves her hand. "Oh, I wasn't that old, sweetie. Caught a rare strand of the flu from one of my patients. Swine flu, I think it was. Or bird. I can't remember. I just know it was something other than plain, ol' human flu. Never could shake it though. So the good Lord called me on home."

"Aw, that's too bad," I say.

Nurse Brenda laughs. "Don't be sorry, sweetie. I love it here. Besides, what's done is done, I always say."

"*Macbeth*," Mr. George says.

Nurse Brenda startles like she didn't know he was there. "What?"

"*Macbeth*," Mr. George says again. "What's done is done. That's *Macbeth*, right?"

Nurse Brenda looks at me and frowns. "What's he talking about?"

"It's a long story," I say. "One that we don't have time for right now."

Nurse Brenda throws Mr. George a courtesy smile and turns her attention back to me. "So, sweetie. You ready to go see your mama?"

Aunt Evangeline joins in the conversation. "Oh, is that why you're here?"

Now, Nurse Brenda looks at Aunt Evangeline like she just noticed she's here too. "Oh my word," she says. "You look so much like little Darlynn. You must be Millie's sister Eva."

"Evangeline Shells," Aunt Evangeline says, extending her hand toward Nurse Brenda. "Pleased to make your acquaintance."

"They called you Eva?" I ask Aunt Evangeline.

Aunt Evangeline frowns. "Millicent called me Eva," she says. "Just like she called your grandmother, Katherine, Kate, and calls herself Millie. She said long names were a waste of time and energy."

Nurse Brenda chuckles. "I do declare. That Millie's a strange one. Never met anyone quite like her."

Aunt Evangeline laughs with her. "Now isn't that the truth?"

Okay. Time to interrupt this party. "Why are you here again?" I ask Nurse Brenda.

Her face lights up. "Oh, yeah, sweetie. I'm gonna take you to see your mama, seeing that I was there when you were born and all. *And* seeing that I know my way around that hospital better'n anyone else here who knows you. So, you ready to go?"

I shrug. "I guess so." I gesture toward the others. "What about them?"

"Life's a party," says Nurse Brenda. "The more the merrier, I always say." She looks over at Mr. George. "Did that Macbeth fellow say that one too?"

Mr. George doesn't look too pleased with her. "I think I'll stay here. I've got work to do." He scowls at Nurse Brenda. "I think a certain red-haired nurse's mansion might need to be *renovated*."

Life's But a Walking Shadow

"Life's but a walking shadow, a poor player that struts and frets his hour upon the stage and then is heard no more."
~ **Macbeth**

"You gotta be real careful in hospitals," Nurse Brenda says in a hushed tone.

We all walk straight through the big sliding glass doors at the entrance, and they don't even open. I guess it would be kind of weird if the sliding glass doors opened, and there was nobody coming through. At least, nobody can see that there's somebody coming through. But here we are, Nurse Brenda, Aunt Evangeline, Leonard, and me, walking right through the glass like it's not even there.

I don't know why Nurse Brenda chose to go through the Emergency entrance. It's totally buzzing, with people going in and out, doctors being paged, and babies crying.

"Why didn't we just go straight to my room?" I ask her. "Seeing that we can walk through glass and walls and stuff."

"Like I said," Nurse Brenda says, without stopping, her thick-soled shoes landing silently on the floor. "You gotta be real careful in hospitals. There're a lot of folks here who can see us."

"Really?" Leonard asks.

"Oh, yeah, sweetie," Nurse Brenda says, strutting down the hallway in her white uniform like she owns the place. "Especially dementia patients. But the folks in emergency are too distracted by the situation at hand. They don't have time to think about anyone but themselves."

Then she stops abruptly. "Everybody! Over here!" she says, hurriedly, herding us against the wall.

Just then, a bunch of hospital people rush by with a white-sheeted body on a stretcher.

Nurse Brenda points. She whispers, "Like her. She's almost one of us now; she knows we're here."

"What do you mean, 'one of us'?" Leonard asks.

Nurse Brenda shushes him.

"And you don't even wanna go near the morgue," she whispers. "So many souls lingering around that place trying to figure out what to do, it'll make your head spin."

Aunt Evangeline gets a dreamy look in her eyes and whispers, "Life's but a walking shadow, a poor player that struts and frets his hour upon the stage and then is heard no more."

The white-sheeted entourage passes us and we continue down the hallway and pass the elevator.

"We'll take the stairs," Nurse Brenda says. "Less complicated than the elevator."

"This is so cool!" Leonard beams, as we walk right through the door leading to the stairway and start floating up.

"Yeah," I say. "It's like we're ghosts."

Leonard waves his hands and says, "Boo-oo-oo."

We're all laughing until we reach the door for the third floor and read the sign: "Intensive Care Unit."

Suddenly, nothing's funny anymore. And I feel like I just got punched in the gut. I don't know if I want to go through that door. I'm afraid of what's on the other side. My body is there, somewhere along those hallways. But I'm here, in the stairwell, with a different body. A spirit body. A body no one else can see except me and other spirit people. It's creepy. Too creepy. Even for someone who's seen the other side.

Nurse Brenda sees me hesitating. She takes my hand. "I'm here for you, sweetie," she says gently. "Let's go see how your mama's holding up."

Words Fly Up

"My words fly up, my thoughts remain below;
Words without thoughts never to heaven go."
~ **Hamlet**

Mama's still wearing her Pizza Hut uniform. But all of a sudden, I don't hate it anymore. I'd give anything right now to smell that onion and bell pepper scent again. But I can't. I can't even touch her. Well, I can. But Nurse Brenda's already warned me against it. She says if we touch somebody, they'll feel it. And they'll know, because a Spirit-body's touch is special. And Earth-bodies know when it's happened, because the hairs stand up on their arms and the back of their necks.

The four of us stand just inside the door, like we're afraid to go any farther. Well, I don't know about the others, but I am. It's bad enough seeing Mama; I surely don't want to see myself.

My body's just a small lump under a white sheet. I can't see my face because a machine is blocking my view. A life-support machine. That's what Nurse Brenda called it. She says I'm brain dead. So technically, I'm dead, because my brain can't tell my body what to do. That's what the machine is for. To breathe for me, because my body doesn't know to do that without my brain telling it to.

Nurse Brenda says the doctors have told Mama there's nothing else they can do. She has to make a decision: turn off the machine and let me go, or leave it on and hope for a miracle. Looks like Mama's over there mumbling up a miracle.

Mama's in the room alone. And she looks so pitiful, hunched over in that chair beside my bed. She's so close that her knees are touching the bed. She has my hand cradled in both of hers as she rocks back and forth, mumbling something I can't understand. Her prayers, I guess.

I've never seen Mama pray before. She said she hated religion. Because of Aunt Millie. But now her eyes are all glossy, and she's chanting prayers faster than Aunt Millie ever has.

Nurse Brenda nudges me from behind, and I know she wants me to go closer. I take a couple of steps then hesitate and shake my head. I'm not ready.

"It's okay, darlin'," Aunt Evangeline whispers.

Her arm slips around my shoulders, and I feel a gentle squeeze. I inch forward a little more, but not enough to see my face. I look around at my support group, and Leonard gives me a reassuring smile.

I inch forward a little more.

Then I see myself, and I want to cry.

A thin line of blood has managed to soak through the huge gauze strips covering my head. And my crusted, dry lips have practically caved into my swollen face. Just this morning, I had longed for purple passion eyelids. Now a huge purple blotch decorates the right side of my face instead.

I hug myself because I'm cold. I didn't know this could happen to Spirit-bodies. But I'm shivering. Then I realize it's not cold, but fear that's making me shake.

"You can go stand beside your mama, sweetie," Nurse Brenda says. "Just don't touch her."

I go over to the bed and stand right next to Mama, longing to throw my arms around her and tell her I'm all right. That I'm not in pain. That I've been to a beautiful place called Paradise. And that I'm with our wonderful Aunt Evangeline. I want to tell her it's okay. Just let me go. Turn off the machine. Let me go back to that lovely place. And be happy for me, so I can go in peace.

I know Nurse Brenda warned me not to, but I just have to touch Mama's shoulder, if nothing else. I have to let her know I'm here. That I'm really alive and well. She just can't see me.

But just as I reach for Mama's shoulder, she drops my Earth-body's hand back onto the bed. She makes a fist and bangs on the arm of the chair hard enough to break it. Then she looks up toward the ceiling and clenches her teeth. "A machine can make her breathe, but you can't? What kind of god are you?" she says.

I reach for Mama. "No!" I plead. "Please don't talk to God like that."

Nurse Brenda grabs me before my hand reaches Mama's shoulder. "Let her be."

Mama's shoulders shake as she begins to cry. "You claim to be all-powerful, but a machine, a little man-made machine, can out-do you."

I'm so scared God's gonna strike Mama down right here and now, and send her straight to hell, just like Aunt Millie said.

"Can't we stop her?" I plead with Nurse Brenda.

Nurse Brenda shakes her head. "She has a right, sweetie. God gave us freewill to say what we want."

Mama drops her face in her hands and begins to cry loudly. "Why do you keep doing this to me? First my mama, now Jimmy Lee? Do you just hate me or what? Am I really that horrible?" she cries out, her voice choking with tears.

Mama releases an angry moan. "Do you have to take everything from me!"

I want to touch her so badly, but Nurse Brenda is shaking her head, telling me no. She says again, "Leave her be. She has a right to be angry."

Aunt Evangeline whispers, "My words fly up, my thoughts remain below; words without thoughts never to heaven go."

I bet that's from Shakespeare. But what did he know? Besides, Mama's not just thinking these horrible things—she's saying them! And I'm afraid. I'm so afraid. For her. I'm so afraid that I turn to Nurse Brenda and beg. "Please! Just let me touch her shoulder."

Nurse Brenda closes her eyes and breathes in deeply. She exhales and says, "Okay."

When my Spirit-body grabs Mama, she jumps.

I hold on to her for a minute, not wanting to let go. But Nurse Brenda tugs on my arm.

I let Mama go.

She's still sobbing, but she seems calmer. She rubs her arms up and down like she's cold. And after a few seconds, her crying stops.

Still rubbing her arms up and down, she gets up and goes over to the window. She closes her eyes, lifts her head toward the ceiling and begins mumbling again. This goes on for a few minutes, until the door of my room flies open.

In walks Aunt Millie, Ms. Shirley, and a man who's dressed like a priest.

The Steep and Thorny Way

"Do not, as some ungracious pastors do,
Show me the steep and thorny way to heaven."
~ **Hamlet**

Mama turns and glares at Aunt Millie for a second. Then with the same fire in her eyes, she nods toward the man dressed like a priest. "Why's he here?"

Aunt Millie marches straight to my bed and stares down at my body. The strange man follows her. And Ms. Shirley is right behind him.

"I brought the chaplain," Aunt Millie announces.

Mama stares at her even harder. Then she stares as equally hard at the chaplain, an old man with his hair slicked down to one side, trying to cover a huge bald spot.

The priest-man stares back at Mama. His eyes are indifferent, his smile non-existent.

Mama's jaw squares. "Why... is he... here?"

"She's dead, Darlynn," Aunt Millie answers. "He's here to perform her last rites."

Mama shakes her head. "We're not even Catholic, Aunt Millie."

"Pastor Lewis is out of town," Aunt Millie says curtly. "And I didn't have time to call anybody else."

Mama's lips fold in. And I can tell she's trying to keep from swearing. Probably because of the priest. "We don't need a priest," she says, her lips barely moving.

Aunt Millie looks up at Mama and narrows her eyes. "You want that child to go to hell like your mama?"

Mama takes a step toward Aunt Millie. "My mama didn't go to hell," she says, her eyes glossing over with tears.

"Psh!" Aunt Millie snaps. She waves her hand. "She didn't go to Heaven either. I can tell you that."

Ms. Shirley places her hand on Aunt Millie's shoulder. "This ain't the time, Millie," she says, her voice cigarette-croaky.

Aunt Millie snatches her shoulder away. "I'm trying to help save this girl's soul. Which is more than I can say for her mama." Then she turns on Mama. "Just because you want to go to hell and be with your mama don't mean this child should have to go too."

Mama's face hardens. She goes over and rises on her toes so she's standing nose to nose with Aunt Millie. "Both you and your priest can go to hell."

Aunt Millie jerks back, looking stunned.

The priest-man stares down at the floor.

Mama says, "Get out of my daughter's room."

Ms. Shirley pats Aunt Millie's shoulder. "Let's go, Millie. Give her a lil' more time."

But Aunt Millie doesn't move, except to shrug Ms. Shirley's hand off her shoulder.

If looks could kill, Mama would be dead right now. But, instead, Aunt Millie calls Mama something worse than she called my friend Felicia's mama. And I feel like my heart just got ripped out.

Aunt Evangeline shakes her head and leaves the room.

Leonard looks at me with sad eyes, and I'm totally embarrassed.

Nurse Brenda holds my hand.

"Let's go, Millie," Ms. Shirley says, grabbing Aunt Millie's wrist. "This ain't about you. It's about saving Jimmy."

Aunt Millie yanks her wrist out of Ms. Shirley's grip and turns on her heels. The priest follows her. But when she reaches the door, she spins around and snatches the bible from the priest's hand. She flips through the bible then narrows her eyes at Mama. "Whosoever shall cause one of these little ones that believe on me to stumble," she reads, "it were better for him if a great millstone were hanged about his neck, and he were cast into the sea."

She slams the bible shut. "May God have mercy on that child's soul," she says. "Because he sure won't have any on yours."

The room suddenly feels ice cold. And I shiver.

But Mama stands her ground. "Get out of my daughter's room," she says to Aunt Millie. "And get out of my life."

Lost Without Deserving

"Reputation is an idle and most false imposition;
oft got without merit and lost without deserving."
~ Othello

Aunt Evangeline comes back into the room, and I can tell that her Spirit-heart has been ripped out just like mine. She grabs me and holds me for a long time.

After which, I pull back and shake my head. "Why did Aunt Millie call her that?"

Nurse Brenda clears her throat. "We'll wait outside." She ushers Leonard toward the door.

Aunt Evangeline releases me from her embrace and turns to Mama, who's again staring teary-eyed out the window. Aunt Evangeline goes over to her and reaches out to touch her, but suddenly changes her mind. She shakes her head and comes back to me.

"Darlynn will be okay," she whispers. "She's strong."

"But why—"

Aunt Evangeline shushes me. She grabs both of my hands in hers and smiles lovingly. Her once sparkling eyes are now dim. "Reputation is an idle and most false imposition; oft got without merit and lost without deserving."

I choke back tears. "It's because of me, isn't it?"

Aunt Evangeline shakes her head. "Not because of you, Jimmy Lee," she says, squeezing my hands. "Because of love."

Confused, I tilt my head to the side.

"Love can make people do irrational things they otherwise wouldn't do with a clear mind," Aunt Evangeline says. "That's something Millicent will never comprehend. Because she's never loved like that."

I hold my breath, fearing that Aunt Evangeline's about to give me a lesson on the birds and the bees. A lesson I'm not ready to hear. I've heard some other girls talking about it. But I try not to listen. Aunt Millie says it's bad. And that's why Mama's going to the hot place.

But Aunt Evangeline doesn't keep talking about it. She simply shakes her head and says, "Millicent will never understand."

She lets go of my hands and goes back to Mama's side. I watch the two of them—Mama in her real body and Aunt Evangeline in her Earth-form Spirit-body—and I see that Mama could've been like Aunt Evangeline if it wasn't for Aunt Millie, always tearing her down. I think about how Mama wanted to go to college and study botany. But she says she couldn't because of me.

Now I know that's not true either. Plenty of girls have babies when they're in high school and still go to college. Something else held Mama back. And that something else was Aunt Millie.

I've asked Mama a thousand times why we won't leave. We could have our own place if she would just keep a job. But she always says Aunt Millie needs us. Seems to me it's the other way around.

Maybe if my daddy hadn't died, he would've married Mama. And things would be different. I would have a family, like Danielle. A daddy who goes off to work every day, and a Mama who stays home to make sure we have everything we need.

But it didn't happen that way. Some fool gunned him down for no reason. Killing him before I was born.

So I'm the only good thing Mama has left. And just to think I was almost selfish enough to leave her makes my heart sick. How could I possibly leave her when I've been given a second chance to live? Mama needs me. I have to come back for her, or Aunt Millie will break her for sure.

I get Aunt Evangeline's attention and motion her toward me.

"I've made my decision," I tell her.

She raises a brow, but she doesn't say anything. I can tell she's torn. She really wants me with her, but she also knows that Mama needs me here too.

"I'm coming back to my body," I say.

She nods. "Your mama needs you."

Aunt Evangeline opens her arms to me, and I fall into them and sob. I want so badly to stay with her. "I won't get to see your theater."

Aunt Evangeline rubs my back. "It's okay, darlin'. It'll be there when it's truly your time to come. I'm not going anywhere."

I sniffle. "I know. But it's so hard to just get to know you then turn around and have to leave you. Who knows how long I'll have to wait to see you again."

Aunt Evangeline strokes my hair. "I'll come visit you, darlin'. Often. And I'll make sure you know I'm there."

"Will I be able to see you?" I ask, sniffling.

Aunt Evangeline shakes her head. "No, darlin'," she says. "Only certain people can see spirits." She smiles sympathetically and says, "And I'm so sorry that you're not one of them, Jimmy Lee."

"Then how will I know you're here?"

"Honeysuckle," Aunt Evangeline answers. "I'll always wear honeysuckle when I come. So when you smell it, you'll know I'm here."

I sigh and suck up my tears.

Aunt Evangeline releases me from her embrace. "Well, let's go get Brenda and Leonard and transport back," she says. "We'll let Chuck know as soon as we get there. He'll have to bring you back to your body, properly."

I take a deep breath and release it in a long sigh. "If my daddy had lived," I say, "maybe he would've married Mama. And things would've been different for us. Maybe Mama would've been a different person if she hadn't had to live with Aunt Millie for so long."

Aunt Evangeline jumps. Her eyebrows come together. "Your da—" She shakes her head and looks at me real funny. "Darlin'," she says, "your father isn't dead. He's still alive. He—". She frowns. "Who told you your father was dead? Millicent?"

"What are you talking about, Aunt Evangeline? My daddy died right before I was born. Mama says somebody shot him."

Aunt Evangeline looks puzzled. "Why in the world would Darlynn say a thing like that?"

The Serpent
Underneath

"Look like the innocent flower,
But be the serpent under it."
~ **Macbeth**

I never thought Mama would lie to me like that. All this time, and my daddy's still alive—living in another city with his wife, a daughter and a son named *Jimmy*. Jimmy Lee Johnson, the Third. If I ever meet him, I'm gonna call him Jimmy Lee Johnson, the Turd.

How could Mama do that to me? After Aunt Evangeline told me that, I just wanted to be left alone.

"I thought you knew, darlin'. I thought you knew," she kept saying over and over.

How could I have known, when my mama's a liar like Aunt Millie said, trying to make herself look like the innocent flower, and Aunt Millie the serpent under it. And to think I felt sorry for her and almost chose her over Aunt Evangeline. Wonderful, sweet, *honest*, beautiful Aunt Evangeline.

After we transported back to Paradise, Nurse Brenda said her good-byes and went back to Heaven for a family gathering at one of her ancestors' mansions. Then I left Aunt Evangeline and Leonard at his gazebo and walked around until I found a gazebo hidden deep in a rose garden.

I was so angry that even the spectacular sunrise didn't help my mood.

Just like Aunt Evangeline had said, the sunset lasted just long enough for me to be satisfied with it. Then it was gone. I couldn't help but wonder if I was the only one who saw it or if every soul in Paradise was content with the sunset at the same time. Anyway, the sunset ended perfectly, and after a brief, but breathtaking twilight, the sun, or something like the sun, rose brilliantly on the other side of Paradise, at just the right time. And I couldn't even enjoy it, because Mama had made me so mad.

I thought right then and there that I should just go find Chuck myself and have him take me back to my body so I could wake up and tell Mama a piece of my mind. Then again, maybe it would be better to go ahead and die and come back as a ghost and haunt her. That would teach her a lesson.

But instead, Aunt Evangeline said to wait until I calm down to make a decision. So I'm just sitting here, watching the sunrise, listening to birds sing, and feeling like crying again. I remember crying once when I got a 76 on an English test, and A. J. called me a crybaby. I wonder what she'd think of me now if she saw how much crying I'd been doing in a place that was supposed to wipe every tear from my eye.

And before I know it, they're just rolling down my cheeks. But I can't help it. My own daddy left me, just walked off, right before I was born. Then my own mama lied and let me think somebody gunned him down for no reason. All this time she had me hating the wrong person, somebody that didn't even exist. When the folks I should really be hating are her and my daddy. For messing up my life.

While I sit and mope, the sunrise turns into a day. The sky is a perfect blue, with no clouds, not even a sun. It's the strangest thing. There's a sunrise and a sunset, but no sun. I'm looking up for it everywhere, but I can't find it anywhere.

I shrug. At least I won't get sunburned.

A little blue bird flies up to me and lands right on the bench beside me. All my short life I chased birds when they landed, trying to catch one. Now one just lands right beside me, stands there on its scrawny legs and watches me pout.

The bird tilts his little head. "Tweet. Tweet."

I smile and say, "Tweet. Tweet," back.

I hold out my hand to see what it'll do. And it flutters right over to me and lands on my hand! I've never held a bird before. Well, not a live one anyway. In third grade, this mean boy named Danny Ray put a dead one in my backpack. And I accidentally picked it up. It was not a happy moment.

"Hello," a man's voice calls out.

I startle, and my bird flies away.

I didn't see or hear anyone coming, but a man is standing a few feet away from my gazebo, *in my secret garden*. He's just staring at me. I don't know what it is with these men in Heaven, but he's wearing slacks and a button-down sweater that make him look just like Mr. George—another Mr. Rogers look-a-like.

His hair is neatly trimmed, and he has a moustache. He's short, no taller than my lying mama. (She's only a couple of inches taller than me—unlike that giant Aunt Millie.) And he's a little thick around the middle, like I used to be.

"Hello," I say timidly.

The man strolls over and stands right in front of me, studying me. A huge smile suddenly spreads across his face.

I squint at him. "Did Chuck send you?"

I'm waiting for him to answer me, but instead, he's just looking at me, smiling, making me uncomfortable. I fidget. He shakes his head, like he's just coming out of a daze.

"Did Chuck—" I start to ask again.

But before I can get my words out, he pulls me up and hugs me.

He lets go of me and holds me back at arm's length and stares and smiles. He's even goofier than Mr. George.

"I'm so happy to finally see you," he says, his eyes misting.

He's freaking me out, so I pull away and put some distance between us. "Should I know you?" I ask.

He shakes his head. "No. You wouldn't know me. You never got the chance."

His smile turns upside-down. "And I'm very sorry about that, Jimmy Lee," he says.

He keeps shaking his head, and I step back a little farther.

"Sorry about what?" I ask cautiously.

His face looks pained. "I'm sorry we didn't do right by you."

My face asks a million questions.

"I'm your great-grandfather, Jeremiah Johnson," he says. "And it's my fault you didn't get to know your daddy."

Acting the Fool

"The fool thinks himself to be wise, but the wise man knows himself to be a fool."
~ **Measure for Measure**

I stumble and practically fall onto the bench.

That's the kind of news you shouldn't tell a person while they're standing up. You should ask them to sit, like they do in the movies, before you just spring it on them that you're the reason they didn't get to know their daddy.

I'm trying not to hate this man, because he's looking so sad and pitiful. I bet that's how Mama's gonna look too when I tell her I know she lied to me.

Mr. Johnson, that's Jeremiah Johnson, who calls himself my great-grandfather, comes over and takes a seat beside me, uninvited. And for the record, unwelcomed. Besides, I was saving that seat for my bird.

I scoot over as far as I can to the other side of the bench. And he better not even think of touching me.

Great-grandpa Johnson shakes his head. "They were both so young," he says. "Jimmy Jr. and your mama. My wife Sophia and I warned them to slow down. To be careful. Love is a powerful thing, and it must be handled wisely."

And I thought A. J. could say some foolish things.

"But they didn't listen," he continues. "They fell in love so quickly and so strong." He shakes his head. "They were only sixteen."

Okay. I might be twelve, but I still know a little bit about the birds and the bees. Why doesn't he just come on out and say it? Mama and Jimmy, the Second, a.k.a. my daddy, got too friendly, then too grown-up, then started acting like married folks, as Aunt Millie likes to say. And like married folks, they made a baby. Except married folks intend to have their babies and raise them together. At least that's what Aunt Millie says.

"We, my wife Sophia and I, had big plans for Jimmy Jr.," Great-grandpa smiles and says.

The way he keeps breaking down all his pronouns for me, he must have been an English teacher.

"He was a smart boy, Jimmy Jr., on his way to college, to study Law."

So was my mama. To study botany.

"I said to him, 'Son, you got your whole life ahead of you. Don't try to run it too fast. Slow down. Take your time. Love will still be there when you're older.'"

He shakes his head. "But he didn't listen."

He twists his face in agony. "He acted like a plum fool."

"So I came along," I say.

He nods. Like he's still ashamed of me.

I don't say anything else, but he's staring at me like he wants me to say something. Instead, I shrug and turn my head.

Great-grandpa Johnson eases over to my side of the bench and places his hand on my shoulder. I don't turn to look at him, though. Instead, I pull away and stand up. He does the same.

He beckons. "Come with me. I want to show you something."

He stuffs his hands into his pockets, lowers his head and starts walking along the path leading away from my secret garden.

We walk along a cobblestone path surrounded by flowers of different kinds, and these I actually know— roses, tulips, carnations, even irises, the one Aunt Millie hates. She never says why. She just says she hates them. But, Aunt Millie hates plenty of things for no reason. Why should flowers be any different?

"Where are we going?" I ask.

"Not much farther," Great-grandpa Johnson answers. He points to a cluster of trees. "It's just up ahead."

We continue on until we reach the cluster of trees. Great-grandpa Johnson enters first, and I follow, even though Mama taught me better than to go anywhere with a stranger.

"Watch your step," Great-grandpa Johnson orders.

And the next thing I know, I'm standing on top of a mountain—like the Grand Canyon or something!

"Wow," I whisper, forgetting that I'm supposed to be mad at the folks who brought me into being. "It's beautiful."

Great-grandpa Johnson smiles and nods.

"Where *are* we?"

"Paradise's version of the Grand Canyon," Great-grandpa Johnson answers.

"Why'd you bring me here?"

"To show you the past."

"Here?" I ask.

"This is a meditation spot," Great-grandpa Johnson answers. "Here you'll be able to open up your mind in order to reflect upon the past."

I get snarky. "I'm only twelve. I don't have that much to reflect over."

"Not *your* past," Great-grandpa Johnson answers. "Your parents' past."

Great-grandpa Johnson sits crisscross applesauce on the ground like we did in kindergarten. I just stare at him. He beckons me to join him.

I sit crisscross applesauce and put my hands on my knees. My thumb and middle finger connect. I hum.

Great-grandpa Johnson shakes his head. "That won't be necessary."

He puts his hands in his lap and closes his eyes.

So I do the same.

Love Is Blind

"Love looks not with the eyes, but with the mind;
And therefore is wing'd Cupid painted blind."
~ A Midsummer Night's Dream

Wow. I can't believe I'm here. At Clark-Cooke High School. Sitting in the auditorium. Watching my mama and daddy.

And Mama's so beautiful. Just like Aunt Evangeline. Smooth copper-tone skin. Not a feature out of proportion. She probably could've been homecoming queen, as pretty as she was.

Too bad cigarettes and stress have done a number on her now.

And look at my daddy, sitting there with his arm around her, probably sweet-talking her.

Great-grandpa Johnson and I stroll down the aisle of the crowded auditorium and look for a seat.

Luckily, we find a spot close enough that we can see Mama and Jimmy Jr.

Boy, this is weird, sitting here in the high school auditorium with all these folks from the past. And it doesn't even feel like a dream. It's like we're really here.

A guy in gray slacks and a starched white shirt jogs up to the stage and does a mic check. He must be the principal because he rattles on and on about a bunch of rules. Then he begins announcing the results of some contest.

"Most likely to succeed: Carrie Hall and Dennis Abram."

"Most likely to end up in jail: Jannis Hollings and Adam Landers."

The auditorium erupts into laughter.

Mr. Gray-slacks-and-white-shirt taps the mic. "Quiet please," he says.

He clears his throat. "Most likely to marry: Darlynn Easton and Jimmy Lee Johnson."

Now that's a joke.

But instead of laughing, the crowd goes wild with hoots and handclapping. My daddy stands up and takes a bow. Mama smiles shyly.

I don't know why she likes him; he's not even cute. Guess Cupid must've shot her with one of his arrows.

But before I have time to think another thought, Great-grandpa Johnson whisks me off, straight through the roof of the auditorium.

"Why'd you do that?" I ask. We sail through the air, right over the school.

"That's all you need to see," he answers.

Wow. I feel like Ebenezer Scrooge, except I'm wearing clothes instead of a nightgown. And I'm peeping into somebody else's past instead of my own.

Okay. Now we land in a park, and it's not the rundown one by Harvey Estates either. It's the nice, well-kept one near Danielle's side of town.

Wow. Mama and Jimmy Jr. are here, too, with a blanket spread out for a picnic.

Ooooh. I bet Aunt Millie doesn't know Mama's wearing those cut-off blue jean shorts. And a tank top, too! Wonder how she got out of the apartment with that on.

Gross. Mama's feeding Jimmy Jr. his sandwich.

I groan. No guy is that special. "He has two hands. Let him feed himself."

Great-grandpa Johnson cuts his eyes at me. "Just watch."

After Mama dabs a napkin on Jimmy Jr.'s ugly face, Jimmy Jr. kisses her right on the lips. Right in the park. For the whole world to see.

Then he reaches into his pocket and pulls out a little black box.

He shows it to Mama. She gushes.

Jimmy Jr. opens the box. Then Mama throws her hands to her mouth and screams so loud the birds fly away.

A ring. He's offering her a ring. Probably something he got at the dollar store.

I cross my arms and glare at them. "I can't believe he had the nerve to give Mama a promise ring."

Great-grandpa Johnson frowns. "Not a promise ring. An *engagement* ring."

"What! An engage—? He can't do that! They're only sixteen! She won't even let me wear makeup till I'm fifteen."

Great-grandpa Johnson doesn't say anything, but his face looks pained.

"They're just kids," I say, my voice panicky. "They can't get married. They can't take that guy seriously. I mean, that whole 'most likely to marry' thing was just a joke, right?"

Great-grandpa Johnson's face is all twisted like he has stomach cramps. "They're not getting married because of that," he says bitterly.

Then I understand. "They have to get married because of me," I say quietly. I can feel Great-grandpa Johnson's accusing eyes burning a hole in my heart. Even after twelve years, he still hates me.

He doesn't say a word. He simply whisks me off again.

Now we're in a place I've never seen before. Somebody's living room. A really nice living room at that. Somehow, even though this isn't real, I can still feel the plush of the dark green carpet under my feet and smell the rosy scent of air freshener. The whole room is spotless—from the glossy white paint on the walls to the shiny wood coffee and end tables. And I wouldn't even think of sitting on that velvety white furniture. But I see Jimmy Jr. and Mama are sitting on it, just the same. And I see Mama's not wearing her teeny-weeny shorts and tank top anymore either. Her belly's too round.

Then two people walk into the room from the hallway. Jimmy Jr.'s parents, I assume. And from the looks on their faces, I don't think they're too pleased with Mama and Jimmy Jr.

Grandma Johnson, Jimmy Jr.'s mama, is all boo-hooing, and Grandpa Johnson, Jimmy Jr.s daddy, looks like he's ready to punch somebody.

"How could you two be so foolish!" he says.

Jimmy Jr. flinches. Mama doesn't budge.

"We're getting married," Jimmy Jr. says nervously.

Grandpa Johnson's face twists. "I'd rather see you dead before I allow that, son."

Then Grandma Johnson really starts bawling.

"I love Darlynn," Jimmy Jr. says, almost mumbling. "And I want to marry her. I want our baby to have my name."

Grandpa Johnson laughs. "Good Lord, boy," he says, talking to Jimmy Jr., but looking at Mama. "Don't be a fool. You don't know anything about love. Besides," he says, turning up his nose at Mama, "you don't even know if that baby's yours."

Now Mama starts crying.

My heart falls into my stomach. "Can we leave?" I ask Great-grandpa Johnson. He shakes his head.

"Look what you've done to your mother," Grandpa Johnson bellows, swinging his arms all over the place. Grandma Johnson dabs her eyes with a handkerchief. They don't even offer Mama a tissue.

Jimmy Jr. grabs Mama's hand and says, "Let's go, Darlynn."

But Grandpa Johnson pushes Jimmy Jr. back down on the fancy sofa then turns to Mama. And with the meanest face I've ever seen in my life, he calls her that name Aunt Millie called her at the hospital and tells her to get out of his house and never come back.

Mama heads toward the door, and Jimmy Jr. jumps up to stop her.

Grandpa Johnson shoves him back. "Let her go, son," he says. "She's not worth it. Don't let her ruin your future."

And Jimmy Jr. sits right back down and allows Mama to leave, her head hanging, sobbing, without a tissue to even wipe away her tears.

Then the whole scene disappears, and we're back in Paradise, at the Grand Canyon.

I'm so mad that steam is coming out of my ears. I jump to my feet and cut my eyes at Great-grandpa Johnson. "My granddaddy was an evil man," I say. "And if I ever meet him, I'm gonna spit in his face."

But Great-grandpa Johnson, still sitting crisscross applesauce, is bawling like a baby.

I stamp my foot. "I mean it," I say. "I'm gonna kill him, too."

Great-grandpa Johnson slowly gets up. He looks me in the eyes and says, "You don't have to kill me. I'm already dead."

You Traitor!

*"When our actions do not,
Our fears do make us traitors."*
~ Macbeth

I fall backward, away from Great-grandpa Johnson. "Wh-what do you mean, you're already dead?" I stammer. I know I'm not entirely flesh and blood anymore, but my hands are shaking like leaves in a storm. And I feel like I'm gonna throw up.

Great-grandpa Johnson is shaking, too. And he's crying really hard. "That was me you saw!" he cries, his face twisted angrily. He shakes his head. "Jimmy Jr. never knew his parents."

I sit on the ground. I can't take this stuff standing up. I fold over, hugging my knees to my chest, not wanting to be here with this man. This horrible man.

He comes and stands right over me. He's stopped his crying, but his face still looks like a virus is eating up his insides. "My son, Jimmy, and his wife Candice were killed in a plane crash when Jimmy Jr. was a baby," he says calmly. "Sophia and I raised Jimmy Jr."

He plops down beside me, uninvited.

"All we ever wanted was the best for him," he says, shaking his head. "So we sent him away. Out of the country. As an exchange student. And forbade him to ever see your mother again. We wouldn't even let you have our name," he says then starts bawling again. "We threatened to sue the hospital if they allowed it," he says, choking on saliva.

I jump up and move away from him. "I don't wanna hear anymore, okay?" I say, waving my hands. "I've heard and seen enough. So you can just go on back to your mansion, or wherever you came from, and leave me alone."

I turn and walk away.

The creep follows me.

"I'm sorry," he pleads.

I turn around quickly, cross my arms, and give him my worst A.J. look ever. "You've made your peace, you traitor," I say. "Now leave me alone and go rest in peace. If you can."

I turn and storm off. Great-grandpa Johnson doesn't follow me this time.

Then I decide I shouldn't let him off so easily. I need to give him a piece of my mind. I stop, spin around, and set my mouth to yell something rude. Instead I scream louder than when I saw those brake lights on that big truck Mr. Gibbons hit.

Instead of Great-grandpa Johnson, I see a horrible creature that looks like something from a scary movie. Its skin is burned crispy black, and it has horns sticking out of the sides of its head instead of ears. Long, jagged teeth hang from its mouth, and its eyes are flaming like fire. But it's wearing Great-grandpa Johnson's clothes!

I turn and run as fast as I can, hurrying along the cobblestone path back to the rose garden, desperate to get back to my gazebo, praying that thing doesn't follow me. I take a quick glance back, and I don't see it anymore. All I see is black smoke.

I slow down and catch my breath, at least what's left of it. I feel like I'm gonna explode. I don't know what to think. My own flesh and blood disowned me before I even had a chance to live. And poor Mama. Now I know why she's so bitter. And I know why she told me Jimmy Jr. was dead. It was easier for both of us that way.

I take one last look back to make sure the Great-grandpa Johnson demon isn't following me. Seeing that it's not, I catch my breath and take my time and head to my gazebo.

I just want to be left alone. I don't want to go back to Earth. Too much sorrow. Too many haters. I don't even want to go to Heaven right now. I just want to stay here in Paradise by myself. In my secret garden. Forever.

But wouldn't you know it? Before I even get there, I see a huge gray blob waiting for me inside the gazebo. And I don't need to ask any questions. Because I take one look at that face, and I know that it's my Grandma Kate.

I sure hope she has something good to tell me. Because Heaven knows, I can't take any more bad news.

The Evil That Men Do

"The evil that men do lives after them."
~ **Julius Caesar**

As I get closer to the gazebo, I know for sure it's her. She's so beautiful, just like Aunt Evangeline. Except, unlike Aunt Evangeline, Grandma Kate's skin—or whatever they call it here—is really dull. Instead of copper-colored, it's gray. A dull, ashy gray. But she's still beautiful. Breathtakingly beautiful.

But she's wearing the drabbest clothes I've ever seen in my life—a crumpled gray dress that's longer than Aunt Millie's Sunday best. Well, at least it goes with her horrible complexion. And she's the first person I've seen here who's completely barefoot. She's sitting, facing the opening of the gazebo, her legs crossed at the ankles, her hands resting at her sides. She's looking around observing things like it's been a long time since she visited Paradise.

Then she spots me walking toward her, and her motions freeze. She stares straight at me, her eyes unmoving, without emotion. And I'm suddenly afraid.

I stop.

"Grandma Kate," I whisper, barely breathing, my heart pounding, my mind a jumble of thoughts.

What's she like? Aunt Evangeline? Aunt Millie? No. She can't be like Aunt Millie. Aunt Millie said she went to the hot place. So that means she's nothing like her.

Aunt Evangeline? Is she kind and sweet like Aunt Evangeline? Is she funny? Does she love that Shakespeare fellow, too?

Grandma Kate answers for herself. She smiles, then stands and opens her arms to me.

My heart melts. And I run to her. I run to her like a little kid who's been lost in a crowd and has just found my mama. I feel like a little kid, too, running so fast that I'm almost floating.

I reach her and collapse into her arms. She's soft and warm. Like a sunny day in the springtime—not what I expected because she looks so dull. And she smells like—the ground. Like *dirt*.

I feel her tremble. And I know she's crying.

We stay that way for a while. Grandmother and granddaughter. Finally meeting. And I'm not sure what I feel.

Grandma Kate releases me from her embrace, but she doesn't let go of me. Her soft hands gently hold onto my wrists.

I've never known anyone to cry and look beautiful at the same time. But she does. Real tears roll from her grayish eyes and flow down her face. But her mouth remains fixed in a smile. And I can't help but smile back.

She pulls me to her again and kisses the top of my head. That's when I notice she's tall like Aunt Millie instead of short like Mama, Aunt Evangeline, and me. I shudder, just a bit, hoping she's not like Aunt Millie in any other way.

"Oh, Jimmy Lee," she says, softly, hugging me tighter. "I've been waiting so long for my little Darlynn to get here." She loosens her embrace and smiles down at me. "But you've come in her place."

A lump fills my throat. Is she disappointed?

She lets go of my arms and takes me by one hand. "Come. Let's sit," she says, guiding me toward the bench in the gazebo.

We sit and she places her arm around my waist and pulls me close to her. Then she laughs slightly. "I never thought I'd get to see my granddaughter before I saw my daughter," she says quietly.

Granddaughter. The word doesn't even sound right because Grandma Kate doesn't look any older than Mama is right now. Actually, she looks younger, like she's twenty-five or something. Like maybe she could be my older sister instead of my grandma.

I muster up the courage to finally say something back to her. "Are you disappointed that I came instead of Mama?"

She laughs gently. "No, Jimmy Lee. Of course not." She leans her head over mine. "I'm just surprised. When I was awakened, I was sure it was time."

I look up at her. "Awakened?"

"Didn't Evangeline tell you?" she asks, looking surprised.

I shake my head. "Tell me what?"

"That I've been asleep," she answers, her forehead wrinkled. "In the Between. I've been there waiting for Darlynn." Her eyes sadden. "I just couldn't move on without her. Without my baby girl," she says softly.

"What do you mean 'asleep'? And where's the Between?"

"Obviously, Evangeline didn't tell you," Grandma Kate says, looking confused. "The Between is where souls rest until they're ready to move on. And since I wanted to wait for my little girl, I was allowed to go there. When I was summoned to come here, I thought it was time."

She hesitates then sighs and says, "I'll admit, I was a little disappointed when it wasn't Darlynn."

I look away from her. "Sorry to disappoint you," I say quietly.

"Oh, Jimmy Lee," she says, grabbing my hand. "I'm not disappointed to see you. I'm happy you're here. It's just that I've waited so long for Darlynn...," she stops and pulls away from me.

She stands and smooths down that hideous gray dress then begins pacing around the gazebo, her bare feet silent against the white floor. "I never really got to see Darlynn, you know? Except for those few minutes after she was born..." Her voice trails off again, and her eyes look far away.

I think about what she just said for a minute then say, "You mean to tell me that neither of my parents got to know their parents?"

She shrugs. "I don't know anything about your father, Jimmy Lee. But I died from a blood clot shortly after I delivered Darlynn." She sighs heavily. "I never even got to hold her to my breast."

Okay. Too much information. Time to change the subject. "Aren't you gonna take me to the Earth-realm?" I ask.

Grandma Kate stops her pacing. "Why?" she asks, tilting her head to one side.

I shrug. "'Cause that's what everybody else did?"

Grandma Kate shakes her head and wrings her hands nervously. She starts pacing again, taking quick steps. After a few seconds, she stops abruptly and turns to me and briskly says, "No."

"But aren't you supposed to show me something?" I ask. "Like, say, the past, perhaps? Or maybe the future, since I've already seen the present and the past. You know, like an Ebenezer Scrooge kind of thing?"

Grandma Kate shakes her head again. "No," she says, wringing her hands. "I...," she pauses. "I can't go back."

She takes a seat opposite me and stares at nothing, her lips sealed tight. She looks down, shaking her head. "I just can't go back," she mutters. "Too much pain."

"You mean the pain from how you died?" I ask.

Grandma Kate shakes her head slowly. "No. The pain and sufferings of life," she says absently.

"But you've been asleep for almost thirty years," I say. "Aren't you curious about what's going on?"

Grandma Kate's face twists into a thousand lines. "We get awakened—summoned—from time to time. When it's necessary," she says, her voice strained. "Even as sleepers we're sometimes called to visit the Earth-realm against our wills. There are things we're forced to see. To be a part of, even if we don't want to."

She shudders and rubs her hands up and down her arms the way Mama was doing when I saw her at the hospital. Her eyes mist up. "I've seen enough," she says sharply.

I go over and sit beside her and put my arm around her shoulders. "It's okay," I say. "You don't have to take me back." I lean into her and rest my head on her arm, trying to imagine what it would've been like to have a real grandmother to share my life with. "You don't even have to tell me about the past if you don't want to."

"Oh, Jimmy Lee, it's not that," she whispers. "I just don't think I can bear to see Darlynn living like that." She shakes her head. "Not if I don't have to."

I straighten up and look at her face. "Like what?" I ask.

Grandma Kate takes a deep breath then lets it out loudly. "Living so sad. So lonely. Living...with Millie," she says, a lone tear rolling down her cheek.

She wipes the tear with the back of her hand. "Millie was right," she says, her voice quivering. "I shouldn't have done what I did. I cursed myself and Darlynn too." She shakes her head. "I cursed us both."

I laugh nervously. "Ah, c'mon, Grandma Kate," I say. "You know you can't believe anything Aunt Millie says."

This time, Grandma Kate laughs—an eerie hollow laugh. "The evil that men do lives after them," she says in a voice so deep that she doesn't even sound like a woman anymore. "Their sins are passed down from one generation to another. From father to son. From mother to daughter. From one generation to the next."

I look up at her and see that her gray eyes have turned completely white, like they've rolled back into her head. Her face contorts and her head drops forward.

I shake her.

"Grandma Kate!" I scream.

But I'm too late. She falls asleep in my arms.

My hands are shaking wildly, but I manage to ease Grandma Kate onto the bench without letting her fall. I hate to leave her, but I have no choice. I rush back and get Aunt Evangeline.

To Thine Ownself Be True

"This above all—to thine ownself be true."
~ Hamlet

By the time we get back to the rose garden, Grandma Kate is gone. Just disappeared.

I look around frantically. "She was right here!" I say, pointing to the bench. "She started talking in this weird, man kind of voice, saying stuff about sins being passed down. Then the next thing I know, she falls asleep."

I hug myself to keep from shaking. I pace around the gazebo, just like Grandma Kate had been doing before she fell asleep.

Aunt Evangeline rubs her hand over the spot where I said Grandma Kate had been lying. "The poor dear," she says. "She went back to the Between. Katherine was never one to handle much pressure."

"But what happened to her body!" I say, my stomach all tied up in knots.

Aunt Evangeline pats my shoulder. "Don't worry, darlin'," she says. "Your grandmother wasn't harmed. She simply transitioned back to the Between."

"What's that?" Leonard asks, his eyebrows shooting up.

"My grandmother's asleep," I say, crossing and uncrossing my arms nervously, feeling like I want to cry. "She's been asleep in this place called the Between ever since she died. She only wakes up when she's summoned."

"Like a séance?" Leonard asks, excitedly.

We both look at Aunt Evangeline. She shakes her head. "No, not like that," she says. "A summons simply means that a messenger angel from Heaven is sent to the Between to awaken those who have chosen to sleep—in case they're needed. Katherine's been awakened on several occasions. Like when your mother was distressed and needed comforting."

I roll my eyes and say, "Like when my daddy left?"

Aunt Evangeline frowns and nods. She's quiet for a moment, then she smiles and says, "But there were also happy times. Like the day you were born."

"You were both there?" I ask.

Aunt Evangeline smiles warmly. "We were both there, my love."

This time I hug myself because of the warmth I feel from Aunt Evangeline.

"Well, how can we get her to come back?" Leonard asks.

Aunt Evangeline shakes her head. "I'm so sorry, darlin'," she says, looking at me. "But I don't think your grandmother is coming back."

I roll my eyes again. "Until Mama gets here, right?"

Aunt Evangeline nods. "And," Aunt Evangeline hesitates then she, too, starts pacing the floor.

"And what?" Leonard asks.

Aunt Evangeline stops pacing. Now *she's* doing the goose-bump rub. She doesn't have to answer Leonard's question, because I can answer him for her.

"My grandma's still afraid of Aunt Millie, just like my mama," I say to Leonard. I hate to say the last part because I feel like a brick just fell into my stomach. But I say it anyway. "And just like me," I mumble, turning my head so Leonard won't see the tears bulging in my eyes.

Aunt Evangeline sits down and motions us to join her. Leonard and I sit on each side of her. She puts her arms around us both.

"Both of you have experienced so much heartache," she says. "You deserve nothing but peace."

She looks over at Leonard. "Leonard, sweetheart, your time has come. You have been rejoined with your earthly father. You have entered your rest."

Then she looks over at me, squeezing me gently. "Jimmy Lee, my darlin', did your mother ever tell you how she got her name?"

"No," I shake my head and whisper.

Aunt Evangeline laughs gently. "When your grandmother was pregnant, I'd whisper to her belly, 'I can't wait to see you, my little darlin'.' So when Darlynn was born, Katherine gave her the name I'd been calling her—Darlynn." Aunt Evangeline stops and frowns. "Millicent, of course, said the name was foolish."

"She has a habit of doing that," I say.

"Indeed she does," Aunt Evangeline says, patting my hand. Then she sighs. "Katherine told you she was cursed, didn't she?"

I look up at her. "How'd you know?"

Aunt Evangeline squeezes my hand. "That's the lie Millicent told her. And it's the same lie she feeds Darlynn, making her think she'll never be more than she is."

"Why would your sister do something so evil?" Leonard asks Aunt Evangeline.

Aunt Evangeline looks Leonard in the eyes and says, "My sister doesn't mean to be evil. She actually thinks she's doing good. She lives with the fear that if everything isn't done exactly to the letter, she'll burn in hell." Aunt Evangeline shakes her head. "She's not evil; she's just confused."

"But, what did my grandma do that would make Aunt Millie call her cursed?" I ask.

"Oh, Jimmy Lee, I do wish Katherine had told you herself," Aunt Evangeline says with a sigh. "But I know she's not coming back here until Darlynn gets here."

This time, I squeeze Aunt Evangeline's hand. "Will you tell me then?"

She nods nervously. "Our own mother, Josephine, transitioned when Katherine was just fourteen," she says. "Millicent was twenty-four, and I was twenty-seven. And, since I had already started my acting career and was on the road, Katherine went to live with Millicent. Unfortunately, Millicent had already become a religious zealot by then."

When Aunt Evangeline pauses, I squeeze her hand to let her know it's okay to go on.

"Sadly, Millicent brain-washed Katherine with all her religious talk, influencing her to become a spinster, just like her." Aunt Evangeline stops and laughs. "I guess I married enough times for all three of us."

"This above all—to thine ownself be true," Leonard says.

Aunt Evangeline smiles. *"Hamlet."* She pats Leonard's hand. "Thank you, dear."

Aunt Evangeline leans back and closes her eyes. "When Katherine was Darlynn's age, just before she turned thirty, she came to visit me in New York City. Against Millicent's will, of course."

Aunt Evangeline releases Leonard and me from her embrace, placing her hands in her lap. "She lived with me for five years before Millicent sent for her, pretending she was ill. Katherine, of course, went back, but she never forgot the freedom she experienced in New York. That's when Millicent began calling her a rebel."

"Like she did Mama," I interrupt.

Aunt Evangeline chuckles. "Did you know your grandmother almost married?" she asks. She shakes her head. "No. Of course you didn't."

"Mama did too," I say.

Aunt Evangeline nods. "Your great-grandfather Jeremiah told you," she pats my hand and says. "But Katherine's suitor didn't get sent away. Katherine changed her mind. Because of Millicent."

"Was my grandma—?" I start to ask, but instead motion with a semi-circle over my stomach.

Aunt Evangeline shakes her head vigorously. "Oh, no, no, no, darlin'. She wasn't. Darlynn didn't come until much later."

"Is that what Aunt Millie had a problem with?"

Aunt Evangeline's face clouds. "Katherine wanted a child, but she didn't want to be burdened with a husband," she says. "And as she began to approach forty, the need grew stronger." Then she pauses. "I really wish she had told you this herself," she says.

Aunt Evangeline takes my hand. "Jimmy Lee, darlin'," she says. "Nobody knows who your grandfather is. Katherine chose an anonymous donor to father her child."

At that moment, it seems all of Heaven and Earth stood still. Not only had my grandmother sinned. But by Aunt Millie's standards, she had probably gone beyond sinning.

"So Aunt Millie said she was cursed," I say quietly.

Aunt Evangeline nods. "And with her dying like that—right after childbirth, she entered Eternity believing she was."

Leonard joins in. "But if she's here, shouldn't she know she wasn't cursed?" he asks.

"She still thinks she was cursed," Aunt Evangeline says.

"And she thinks the curse is still on Mama," I say quietly.

Aunt Evangeline squeezes my hand. "God doesn't make mistakes, Jimmy Lee," she says. "You came here for a reason, you know."

"Yeah," I say sarcastically. "I came here because Mr. Gibbons thought he could talk on a cell phone, drink Red Bull, and drive a school bus all at the same time."

Leonard laughs, but Aunt Evangeline doesn't.

"You came here to help your mother, Jimmy Lee," she says.

I stop laughing and look at her. "I did?"

"Don't you see? You can move on now. And you can help Darlynn move on too. Remember what Leonard told me?"

I nod and say, "Yeah. Something about being true to yourself."

"This above all—to thine ownself be true," Leonard says.

Aunt Evangeline smiles. "You don't have to let Millicent bully you anymore with her lies."

"Nor A. J.," Leonard pipes in.

"I won't," I tell him.

Then Leonard frowns. "Jimmy Lee," he says, hesitantly. "There's something you need to know about Danielle, too."

I shake my head and give him a reassuring smile. "It's okay," I say. "I already know."

Leonard releases a breath and smiles.

Aunt Evangeline gives my hand another gentle squeeze. "You'll find your true friends in time, darlin'," she says.

I laugh and say, "You know, just yesterday— Paradise days, that is—I was afraid of dying twice. But now that I'm no longer afraid of dying, I think I'm ready to live. To truly live."

Leonard peers toward the west and realizes the sunset of the second day is almost over. His face looks pained, but I know he's still happy for me.

"So, you've made up your mind, then?" he says.

"Yes," I say, nodding. "I've made up my mind."

Aunt Evangeline smiles. And I know I've made the right decision.

The Devil Can Cite Scripture

"The devil can cite scripture for his purpose."
~ **The Merchant of Venice**

We didn't have to go look for Chuck. As soon as the sun peeped over the eastern horizon, he showed up. In full classic Hawaiian-style fashion. Pineapple and palm tree shirt, green cargo shorts, and orange flip-flops—to match his newly colored hair.

"Well, well, well, Little Miss, I heard you have some good news to tell me," he says as he struts toward me.

I tilt my head to one side. "How did you know already?"

Chuck holds out his hand, and a little red bird flies straight to it. "Let's just say a little birdie told me."

The bird flaps off, and Chuck comes over and puts his arm around my shoulders. I jump. "I thought you said I was Earth-contaminated."

"You are," he says. "I'm building up my immune system before I take you back." He steps away from me and shudders. "You can never be too careful in hospitals."

"All right, Chuck," Aunt Evangeline waves her hand and says, "enough with the small talk. Let's get Jimmy Lee back where she belongs, so she and her mother can move on with their lives."

Chuck throws up his hands. "Hey, she's the one who couldn't make up her mind."

Leonard extends his hand toward me for a shake. "I'm gonna miss you, Jimmy Lee Easton," he says.

Instead of shaking his hand, I grab him and hug him. I think I feel him shiver. "I'm gonna miss you too, Leonard George," I say in his ear. "And I'll make sure I tell everyone at school that you really are in a better place. And I'll tell them how happy you are too."

Leonard steps back and beams. "Hey, you could speak at my funeral!"

Chuck steps in and interrupts. "Dude, did you see her on that hospital bed?" He waves toward me. "Little Miss here won't be speaking at any funerals any time soon. Her mortal form has a lot of recovering to do."

I wince. I had forgotten about that. I'm all banged up on Earth. Who knows how long I'll be in rehab.

Chuck shoots me a sympathetic look. "Don't worry, Little Miss. I've spoken to the Folks In Charge on your behalf. They've promised a speedy recovery." He shoots another look over at Leonard. A different look. "But not speedy enough to attend your boyfriend's funeral."

"He's not—" I start to say until I look into Leonard's eyes. Of course he's not my boyfriend, but he's still my friend. He died trying to save my life. *Greater love has no one than this, than to lay down one's life for his friends.* (Hey, I didn't always sleep in Sunday school.)

So in classic movie form, I throw my arms around Leonard's neck and give him a kiss—right on the lips. "Thanks for saving my life," I say.

Aunt Evangeline catches him before he hits the ground.

We all have a good laugh then Chuck takes my hand. "You ready?" he asks.

I look over at Aunt Evangeline and see tears in her beautiful eyes. Leonard looks away so that I can't see his. I bite my lip to fight back my own tears. I shake my head and whisper, "Not really. But I know Mama needs me."

Chuck gently pats me on the back. "You're a brave girl, Little Miss. And Mr. George is building a special mansion for you right beside your aunt's," he says. "It'll be waiting for you, no matter how long it takes you to come back."

I can no longer hold back. I let the tears flow and run over to Aunt Evangeline. "I'm gonna miss you so much," I say, sobbing.

Aunt Evangeline holds me tightly. "I'm gonna miss you too, darlin'," she whispers. "And remember," she says, pulling back but keeping her hands on my shoulders. "Even the devil can cite Scripture for his purpose." She winks. "Don't let my sister bully you."

"I won't," I say, smiling.

It's hard, but Aunt Evangeline releases her hold on me and stands next to Leonard. She takes his hand

and says, "Your father will be here any minute to escort you in, dear Leonard." She sighs. "We should probably head to the waterfall now."

Having to watch Aunt Evangeline and Leonard leave, I feel like I'm going to burst inside. But I know this is the way it has to be. I know Aunt Evangeline is right. My near-death was not just an accident. It was a lesson. And I have to go back and take what I've learned to Mama, and possibly Aunt Millie too.

Chuck takes my hand. He doesn't say a word. He doesn't have to. He smiles at me, and we float away.

"Visit soon, Aunt Evangeline," I whisper.

A Man Can Die but Once

"A man can die but once."
~ **King Henry IV Part 2**

When Nurse Brenda took us back to the Earth-realm, it was almost like a dream. A kind of sleep state. One minute, we were in Paradise, and the next, we were on Earth. But not this time. Chuck has to show off.

We soar through a place called The Next. And it's beautiful. It's not where the planets are, but it's a place full of magical creatures, giant mountains, lush flower gardens, and the clearest lakes mankind has ever seen.

"What's this place for anyway?" I call out as we swish through the air.

Chuck calls back, "That's for me to know, and for you to find out!"

When I look over at him, his face is all contorted from the wind. "That's what I'm trying to do!" I say back.

"You'll find out when you come back—officially."

"Guess I'll just have to wait till then," I say.

Chuck winks, or tries to anyway. "Trust me, Little Miss," he says. "This place is to die for."

Chuck slows down so I can enjoy the view. We slowly soar over a mountain, and I think I see sheep grazing on the grass. It's just like the movie *Heidi* that our fifth-grade teacher showed us. It was one of my favorite movies ever, and, for a moment, I wished I was Heidi, living on a mountain. I look over at Chuck again. "Can't you at least give me a hint?" I say, my voice pleading.

Chuck sighs. "Let's just say you'll definitely get to come back to this place one day in the far future. The far, far future," he says, winking again.

"When I die officially, right?"

Chuck smiles. "A man can die but once, sweetheart," he says.

I accept his answer and keep my mouth shut. We soar over a beautiful field filled with golden flowers— sunflowers—to be exact. Mama's favorite.

Mama. Just thinking about her makes my heart happy. I can't believe it was just this morning that I wanted to get away from her, and now I can't wait to see her. I laugh to myself when I think about how Chuck told me only three hours have passed on Earth, but three days have passed in Paradise. It feels like I've been separated from Mama forever. I can't wait to see her again and tell her how much I love her.

And as if on cue, Chuck snaps his fingers. And like something out of the Twilight Zone, we're zapped straight out of The Next and into the Earth realm— right into my hospital room.

And there's Mama, still standing by the window, just like we left her.

Chuck and I stand by my bed, and he squeezes my hand. He smiles and nods. "It's time, Little Miss." Surprisingly, he leans over and kisses me on the cheek. He smells like coconut.

"I'm gonna miss you," I smile and say.

Chuck shakes his head. "No, you won't," he says without smiling.

And I can't help but laugh. He motions toward the bed. "Go on," he says. "Hop in."

And I do.

And it feels really weird, because I immediately fall asleep.

The Sleep of Death

"For in that sleep of death what dreams may come."
~ **Hamlet**

I'm back in my bed again, in the room that Mama and I share in Aunt Millie's apartment in Harvey Estates. And it feels good, even if the mattress does sink a little in the middle. The covers are pulled up over my head, and I don't want to move. But I hear Mama's voice, so I know I have to.

"Get up, Jimmy Lee Easton! RISE and shine! And SHINE and rise!" she yells.

My heart sinks. It was all a dream. Only a dream. I didn't go to a place called Paradise. And there is no Aunt Evangeline or Chuck or Grandma Kate. And poor Leonard is still Poop Boy, unwashed and grimy with yellow teeth.

I moan. I don't want to get up. It's the same old thing. Nothing's changed.

Then I hear Mama scream.

I jerk up from my pillow, but my body doesn't move. It's heavy and stiff. I open my eyes, but they only open slightly. My eyelids are so heavy.

That's when I see her—Mama in her Pizza Hut uniform, tears streaming down her face. And through the tiny slit in my eyelids I can see that we're in the hospital—my hospital room!

"Mama!" I try to say, but all I do is moan. Then I remember what Chuck told me about recovery, and I realize I might not be able to talk just yet.

But without a doubt, I can smell. And right now, all I smell is the unmistakable scent of honeysuckle. Aunt Evangeline. She's already come to reassure me. And I know everything will be okay. Mama and I will both be all right. And we'll live. We'll both really *live*.

I always thought it took courage to die. Now I know, dying is easy, but it takes real courage to live.

I squint at Mama through the narrow slits my eyelids make. She's crying, laughing, and calling for a nurse all at the same time. And she's beautiful. Just like Aunt Evangeline. Beautiful on the outside and within.

And I love her to death.

About the Author

LINDA WILLIAMS JACKSON is the author of award-winning middle grade novels centered around some of Mississippi's most important historical moments. Her first book, *Midnight Without a Moon*, which is set against the Emmett Till murder, was an American Library Association Notable Children's Book, a Jane Addams Honor Book for Peace and Social Justice, and a *Washington Post* Summer Book Club Selection. Her second book, *A Sky Full of Stars*, the sequel to *Midnight Without a Moon*, received a Malka Penn Honor for an outstanding children's book addressing human rights issues and was a Bank Street College Best Book of the Year. Her third work of historical fiction, *The Lucky Ones*, was inspired by Robert Kennedy's 1967 Poverty Tour of the Mississippi Delta and is loosely based on the author's own family's experiences. *The Lucky Ones* was recognized by *Good Housekeeping* magazine as one of the best 50 kids' books of all time. Additional accolades for *The Lucky Ones* include Mississippi Institute of Arts & Letters Youth Book Award Winner, Foreword Reviews Indies Award Winner, New-York Historical Society Children's History Book Prize

Finalist, Common Sense Media's Best Six Kids' Books of 2022, *Week Junior Magazine* Best Seven Kids' Books of 2022, Cooperative Children's Book Center Best Books of the Year, and a Bank Street College Best Books of the Year.

Southern born and Southern bred, **Linda Williams Jackson** is proud to still call Mississippi home.

Visit her online at:
www.lindajacksonwrites.blogspot.com

Made in the USA
Coppell, TX
01 February 2024

28478798R00115